The
Book of

and the ring
that scratched
the face of
truth

Spunky Collins

The author would like to thank Wheatmark staff acquisitions manager Grael Norton for his excellent guidance, support and know-how; editor Michael Lopez-Gaiuranos for his insightful vision; account manager Lori Sellstrom and graphic artist Hayley Love. A warm thanks also goes to Francesca Butler and Andrea Dannegger for their support and everyone else who has served as inspiration for this book.

The Book of O: And the Ring that Scratched the Face of Truth

Published by Wheatmark®
610 East Delano Street, Suite 104, Tucson, Arizona 85705 U.S.A.
www.wheatmark.com

ISBN: 978-1-60494-454-9
LCCN: 2010925975

Book and cover design: Pamela Gehrig

Dedicated to the pursuit of knowing ourselves for who we really are.

CONTENTS

INTRODUCTION

The world is changing … yet humanity sleeps. They are so caught up in their self-inflicted sufferings—greed, ego, fear—that they don't even know of the chaos they're creating or the joy they're missing. If humanity were awake, they would sense the evolutionary shift. They would recognize their self-defeating ways and begin to reinvent their every thought and their every action. They could heal their wounds. They could even live a life of bliss. Alas, perhaps that's just too easy. Perhaps suffering is best, to bear witness to the experience, before an awakening is possible, and then maybe, maybe they'll see the light. But what are the chances?

What of the choices of humanity … will they choose to evolve to ensure a better tomorrow for the sake of all or will the antics of modern man—the pursuit of money, power, war—prevail?

Time will tell.

Diary excerpt, May 2010, O.

PLACE OF ORIGIN

The city of Home is a midsize urban town that lies in Maine's Highlands somewhere between Manson and Harmony. It's a fashionable place with a rich cultural heritage populated by hip, image-conscious extreme types and overachievers, particularly in the pharma and banking industries. The Mony River, running through its center, allows for a quiet place of contemplation or sports, whatever your pleasure—perhaps even a stolen kiss. The river, one of Home's main attractions, helped land the town on *The New Yorker's* list of the fifty most desirable places in the United States to live.

Home, whose slogan "Home Sweet Home" can be found on the local license plates, is a comfortable self-proclaimed green town with an active city center and nightlife, sprinkled with a selection of nouveau haunts to flaunt whatever it is one feels like flaunting. Consuming is the local pastime, though diametrically opposed to being green; they hope no one's keeping score. It's a reputation they're endeavoring to change as bicycles multiply like rabbits and cars take a backseat to the preferred two-wheeled form of transportation. The surrounding suburbia offers everything one could desire in a safe community lifestyle, with modern conveniences on the cutting edge of the millennium; one need only think about what that could be, and sure enough … it's there.

Her world had come undone. There was a tear in the fabric of her knowing.

O[1]

A salty tear rolled down O's cheek in slow motion. She stuck her tongue out to catch it and prevent it from smearing the black ink of her note. O folded the white piece of paper and tenderly placed it on one of the pillows of their bed. Closing the front door behind her, she left their house for the last time.

Disillusioned, ○ realized her life was not quite going the way she had planned.

(Eighteen Months Earlier)

That bloody twitch was back. Tortured three times this week already, ○'s left eye twitched nonstop. Too much time at the computer, perhaps? New glasses could solve the problem, but … it was doubtful.

○ was restless. Her entire inner being itched, in a place of unknown origins.

It was a powerfully disturbing energy raging through her veins—indescribable, unquenchable. Her body craved something—she didn't know what. The fear of losing self-control percolated within. She felt a palpable danger of doing something she might regret. What was this feeling of emptiness deep inside? She couldn't define it or pacify it. There was an essence of sadness to it, but over what? Where does one begin to find the answers to a problem unknown to its owner? Could it stem from a foreboding sense of the future?

"I've got to get out of here!" ○ cried out loud. Filled with anguish, ○ grabbed her solar iPod and, like a thoroughbred out of its stall, blasted out of the house at full speed. Running was her only savior; running to hide, like the hunted rabbits in the Fine Frenzy song playing to her stride on the radio. But how long could one hide from the truth? ○ would soon find out, and on that day her future would depend on the courage she had to change the course of her life.

Her feet landed heavy on the pavement. Just like her thoughts—heavy. Was her marriage failing or was she just restless? How did you know if something was really wrong or if you were just making it all up in your head? She vacillated between thoughts of love and divorce. It wasn't for the lack of love in her marriage. ○ loved her husband. But there was a growing feeling of unrest, of something she did not yet know, at least consciously. The signs were all there—signs that were also taking a physical toll on her such as stomach problems and IBS—but like most people, she was simply not aware enough to read them. She lived in denial, just like she lived in denial about her body's growing hunger for sex.

X and ○'s sex life had never been a highlight. There were other things to build their relationship upon, like … accumulating things. Things that made them feel better about being a couple and about life in general in an ego-based, greed-centered society of conspicuous consumption where enough simply wasn't. Perhaps it was even the material world that contributed to the source of her emptiness.

At forty-two, O was convinced her sexual prowess was over, and she had willingly resigned herself to a sexless marriage. O and neglect were becoming well-acquainted bedfellows. Of course, the numerous suitors of her past remained in secret memory. With a captivating charm, almond-shaped hazel eyes and a figure that could stop traffic in her arsenal, O hardly had trouble attracting the opposite sex. Her sexually charged adventures were as hot as the color of her long red hair, which she blamed for the collection of unreliable artist types who inevitably pursued her. It was the same hair she once cursed for its deviance from the norm, for which a bottled duplicate didn't exist, which had since become her treasure. After all, it was the first thing that had attracted X to her the day they met. He'd always had a weakness for redheads. Blonds were too ubiquitous for his taste. O was his ruby, his *Gem*, as he affectionately called her.

But things change in the realm of passion. O could live without sex at this point in her life, or so she thought, but her body was telling her another story … only she hadn't connected the itch with the truth yet. That would come soon enough.

O loved X and that was all that had mattered until now. But this could soon be challenged as O discovered that love's archrival turned out to be happiness. Was this a trade-off she was willing to endure, and if so, at what price? She had sworn to herself on her wedding day to marry only once, and this pact she intended to keep—life, however, followed a path of its own without asking for permission.

The trail of self-denial seeps like poison through the veins.

X was out chasing the elusive white ball on the green as ○ began to prepare omelets and potatoes for the two of them for dinner. The sizzling sound of eggs in the hot skillet brought back memories of the morning X had prepared eggs after their first night together. Though his cooking was a disaster, it was a magical time in their relationship. Everything was so new. Breakfast started as a picnic on the living room carpet and ended in a love-making marathon on the kitchen floor (never to be matched again).

X and ○ had met at an art exhibition given by a mutual friend. His long legs and intense blue eyes had first captured ○'s attention, but his sense of humor won her over. He still made her laugh. He had a quiet reserve that intrigued her and gave her cause to wonder what really made him tick. Oddly enough, she still wondered about that.

X was captivated with ○ right from the very start, asking more questions than a sleuth in a murder case. He later confessed he wanted to get under her skin to feel her emotional world. He was intrigued by her petite size and strength of character. He loved the sound of her laugh and endeavored to encourage it whenever the occasion arose. He wanted to know everything about her: what brought her joy, what made her sad, her aspirations and her fears, what she looked like in the mornings, and what she wore to bed. ○ found the intense curiosity of a man for a woman utterly seductive and most often underestimated by the majority of men as an effective strategy of seduction. Being "investigated" by the intriguing figure that X was to her then made her feel special; it was an excellent boost for her self-esteem.

Their love grew quickly, and ○ fell hard. After a short courting period, their future became clear. ○ knew, however, that being a doctor's wife meant sacrifice—long nights without him, cancelled plans, being alone—but she was a willing candidate. The financial security that came with it fed ○'s need, having struggled financially most of her life. X was loving and very generous, often bringing ○ unexpected gifts of flowers and jewelry. He took a genuine interest in her devotion to her career and environmental causes and was a good sounding board for her ideas at work, always asking just the right questions to help her realize her projects.

Of course, being married to a prominent doctor had advantages other than material comforts, although as time wore on the sacrifices began to overshadow the prestige. But ○ was a fighter and refused to give up so easily. She found activities to keep herself occupied, such as running and volunteering for the local ecological society. Alone time enabled ○ to study art history and go hiking in the forest. The savored moments with X, consequently, became that much more precious and their time apart that much more painful … eventually, too painful.

○'s mind shifted back to the present, as dinner was about ready. She set the table, lit the candles, and opened a bottle of French Chardonnay. Looking at the clock, she figured X should be done at the club and walking through the door any minute.

"Nice shot, Doc," called V across the green to X.

"Thanks. I'll get my handicap down yet." X smiled at his clever reading of the hole, which had won him his second birdie.

"Another great round, V; let's hit the clubhouse for a cold one. Shall we? I'm loving these perks Medy keeps throwing my way."

"Yeah, what you're doing to keep getting them is what I want to know," asked V, searching for a real answer.

"Well, buddy, let's just say their sales reps are very good at what they do," X said, letting out a smug chuckle of self-content.

Well, what did one expect him to do? With sales reps offering great golf packages, not to mention other perks, why shouldn't he take advantage of their generosity? X put in more than his share of hours as a doctor at the city's most prominent hospital. He'd certainly earned the right to enjoy some time off. Besides, the drugs they wanted him to push were for the benefit of his patients. With all the drugs on the market, who had time to keep up with them, anyway? That's what the reps were for: to keep him informed. Medy was one of the most reputable pharmaceutical companies of all the big pharma boys, which put X's mind at ease. He was confident he could trust their recommendations.

The Medy golf perks were one of X's greatest passions, next to his "male bonding" nights out. X coveted his playtime, something that followed him from his youth. His parents came from old money, which afforded X many luxuries as a young man, such as playing golf at the most exclusive country club in Home. But when he was twenty-two, his parents changed the course of his playboy lifestyle and insisted he pursue a profession worthy of the family name. At the head of his class, X was intellectually gifted but only applied himself when necessary. Granted, X had a talent for biology and even liked it to some degree, but he could think of less consuming jobs that would allow for more playtime. As he went through the motions at a job that robbed his soul through perpetual stress and back-to-back sleepless hours dealing with lives on the edge of death, the need to sugarcoat his private time became more and more of a priority. His profession rendered his motto, "take the path of least effort," null and void.

X's cell phone rang, a reminder that ○ was at home waiting for him.

"Hi, Gem. Yes, sorry, I know I said I'd be back in time for dinner, but our round went a bit long. I'm just finishing up and should be home in about an hour."

○ sat alone at the dinner table staring at the meal in front of her, her appetite waning. Burning with frustration at being left alone yet again, ○ resisted the urge to nosh on her favorite feel-good foods, Dutch chocolate and deviled ham, and opted instead to extinguish the undesirable energy building up inside her. ○ prepared her gym bag and without further delay was out the door.

"Hi, O!" called B from the step climber. "I figured you'd be here working out that cute bod of yours." B, a successful businesswoman by day and self-professed Love Goddess by night, hid nothing of her buxom figure bouncing from breasts to bottom in full motion to the rhythm of her stepping. Her thick brunette waves were piled high upon her head. Working out was a foreign activity for B, who preferred more interactive exercise with the opposite sex to climbing stairs, but O's persistence in advising B on how best to balance her bottom half with her top paid off.

"Hey there, B," called back O. "Yeah, I have to protect my best assets, if you know what I mean." At five-four and 114 pounds, O had little to worry about.

"Where's your man? Is he coming tonight?" asked B.

"No, he's playing golf," replied O in a pretense of nonchalance.

"Good. We can take our time then and have a drink afterward," suggested B.

Just then Mr. S sauntered by—confident strut, impressive broad shoulders, sexy bald-head. His hind parts weren't too bad either.

"Hi, O; nice to see you." S smiled and headed for the arm machines.

"Hi, S," O responded, blushing. "Nice to see you too."

B's mouth dropped open. "You know that guy?" she asked in an envious whisper.

"Well, I wouldn't say I *know him* know him, but he's been coming here for a couple of years, and we often run into each other in town. I do know that he comes from a long line of bankers, his family being one of the most prominent on this side of the Mony."

"Oh mercy me, I feel an orgasm coming on," declared B without apology while fanning herself with her hand as S walked away.

B smiled that enchanting temptress smile that never failed to capture a new lover blind to her love 'em and leave 'em attitude.

"Yeah, me too," O said under her breath, without thinking. "I mean … you know what I mean … ha!" O laughed at herself, realizing she'd revealed more about her private feelings for S than she'd intended. "And you could have more of those orgasms, B, if you came to the gym more often," teased O.

Truth be told, O was unavoidably drawn to S. There was something about that sympathy/strength dichotomy of S's shaved head that intrigued her. Curious, thought O, to be devoted to X as she was and still be so drawn to another man. S was challenging O's perhaps overly naïve understanding of the heart under contract to marriage. No matter how hard she tried to deny the emotions he stirred, he still stirred them, unquestionably.

She watched him out of the corner of her eye as he mounted the arm press machine. There was such intensity about the way he closed his eyes and concentrated. *He's got to be a good lover,* thought O in silent contemplation.

"Mama, he's sexy, don't you think? I'd like to lick his belly!" exclaimed B unabashedly.

O shot B a playful look of disgust. It was exactly that kind of blatant honesty that made B so endearing. She said things as she felt them, allowing others to feel comfortable enough to do the same. It was somehow liberating, and it was that which O yearned to be around and so loved about her friend B. Their long talks laid the truth out on the table in the most satisfying way. If only O could be more like that, without constant constraint or self-assessment. It was only with B that O felt free enough to share her unedited thoughts. O could always rely on an honest assessment from B whenever she needed a sounding board.

"So tell me, what have you been up to, B?" inquired O curiously. *No doubt the usual,* she thought to herself. B, the Love Goddess, felt it her duty to rescue the male population from sexual deprivation, unfortunately at the cost of her own self-worth, not to mention the broken hearts and lives of her trail of suitors. Men *in need* flocked to B, sensing her caretaking abilities, which she had developed at the ripe old age of seventeen when she was forced to take care of her three younger siblings. B neglected to consider, however, the consequences and hurt that inevitably followed her carefree style of love, as the needs of others always took precedence over her own. All of O's advice and consultations over the years had never heeded much return on her investment. B still hadn't learned to set her boundaries.

"Well, let's see … I've been working my ass off, mostly. I'm tired all the time, stressed out, and to tell you the truth, I could really use a nap and an orgasm and call it a day," she said dryly. "Oh, yeah, and I just got promoted to head of the global marketing division at Medy."

"Hey, congratulations, B! That's great! Well, then, why don't we celebrate this weekend?"

"Thanks, but celebrating is not what I have in mind. I feel like such a hypocrite, O. I have to confess this to someone before I explode."

"Confess what? I'm all ears," responded O in a hushed tone.

"Here I am, sitting pretty at the top of one of the biggest pharma companies as one of few female executives in my field, earning a ransom, and I can't stand myself for being a part of this nasty game of low morals and no ethics, where unmentionable activities seem to be becoming the norm. I honestly didn't expect this when I started in the field years ago. I was so green and saw so much promise in this company. Blind is what I was. I thought Medy was one of the good guys. I guess we see what we want to see, don't we? The higher the rung on the ladder, the more privy to dirt you are. Employees who've devoted fifteen to twenty years of service to the company are being laid off for the pure and simple reason that the numbers look good and the CEO looks like a hero when the fourth quarter reports come out. It makes me sick, O, and that's just the tip of the iceberg. Do you know there are companies, which shall remain nameless, that have bribed the FDA to release drugs to the market that have been proven to have major life threatening consequences? Then these drugs are pushed on ignorant doctors, too overworked to know better, and they give them to innocent patients. All this in the name of *profit!* Recovering the costs of research outweighs the importance of people's lives. Money is the only bottom line in this game, O, and I'm stuck in the middle of the whole damn thing."

"Well, just quit then. You don't need this kind of stress. And don't tell me you're sticking it out for the money, because that puts you right up there with the rest of the money mongers," chided O.

"Well, hold on there a minute, cowgirl; it's not quite that simple. I have a career to think about. Sometimes I hate myself for that thought, but … there it is. So the only way to remedy that is … to get naked! Tomorrow I have a date with a gorgeous man I met at one of our seminars. I'll let you know what happens."

"B, I don't want to hear about how you wish you had someone to hold you and care for you and love you. You're just setting yourself up, yet again, to get hurt and used!" O knew the scenario all too well. Over the course of their fifteen-year friendship B had cried to

O again and again for comfort and consultation, suffering from a broken heart, as did her lovers.

"Don't worry so much about me, O! I'm a big girl who has no interest in a serious relationship. Having fun and getting my jollies is my primary concern. So I'm off; gotta go home and do my nails and shave. See you later sweetie; toodles."

O was helpless to the cause. B was a dynamic, take-control kind of woman in a finely wrapped package. She knew no strangers as she greeted both men and women alike with the warmth of her smile. Her idea of free love, no strings attached, was meant with all good intentions, but she ignored one important factor—the heart had another agenda.

Self-destruction—it's a hard habit to break, until it's almost too late.

O³

O sat in the living room in her favorite organic cotton sweats and socks, sipping a glass of Bordeaux and painting her nails red as X prepared for his escape into his mysterious night-life. Like the stimulus-response technique used in training animals, it was the dreaded sound of X's boot heels against the wooden floor that made her cringe every time and sig-

naled to ◯ she'd be spending another night alone. This was the salt in the wound of her marriage. This was it—the threat that could shatter the dream of a life together with the one and only man she'd ever marry. On a scale of one to ten, ◯'s frustration level was at a nine and climbing. The unending routine of nights spent alone till early morning hours had worn her down over the years. The constant worry over when he'd return and what if something bad happened was carving a valley through her heart. And every time she'd try convincing herself that it was a minor detail in the history of their happy marriage. Sometimes her self-persuasion worked, but most of time it didn't. Yet ◯ persisted in applying the bandage of her denial to simulate the happiness she once knew. As her state of contentment slowly sifted through her unconscious fingers, she still convinced herself it was a temporary state of affairs. She only had to figure out what it was her heart and soul so desired that perpetuated this unending hunger for fulfillment. What was she searching for?

"◯, honey, I'm running late so I've got to go, but maybe tomorrow we can catch a movie," placated X, hoping to ward off any negative backlash before his departure. She remembered the last two times he'd said that and then promptly cancelled. He was too tired from his night out to keep his word.

X glanced down at what ◯ was doing. "Red nails? What's that mean?" he asked, surprised. "You never paint your nails red." He found the color very erotic.

"Yeah, I know. I just felt like it, that's all," she shrugged. Indeed, it was a deliberate act, partly out of defiance to him for leaving her alone again and partly out of her need to amuse herself with the secret desire to appeal to any male onlookers. The red served as a signal of the raging emotions bleeding out from under her skin. It was almost cathartic for someone who preferred French manicures.

"Where're you going?" asked ◯ casually, as though accepting her fate of being left alone yet again on another Saturday night. X wore his usual uniform—navy bomber jacket over an untucked white shirt and torn jeans. X's style of dressing had morphed from his preppy days of the past into sloppy chic. It captured the look of what his colleagues considered the *modern man*.

"I'm meeting the boys for a bite, and then we're going to Teez for a few drinks. Don't worry, I won't be too late," promised X. He willingly offered reassurance to her that he wasn't woman-hunting during his nightly outings, as he regularly proclaimed his innocence without provocation. "I love you, Gem." With a loving kiss and a pat on her bum, he was out the door. Such nights with the boys were holy.

○ brushed off the negative emotions that were forcing their way up through her solar plexus and into her throat. She actually enjoyed her nights alone watching DVDs—at least that's what she kept telling herself.

And so the story went, over and over again. But ○ was set on allowing X his "de-stressing" time with his buddies, knowing full well that to take that away from him would send their marriage into a tailspin. X was a nightrider, as ○ fondly thought of him, preferring to live the day into the night rather than the other way around. There was no changing that; thus she allowed it. She was convinced that her open-handed style of love was the right choice. ○ knew X loved her as deeply as he was capable of loving anyone, however limited that was. That had been reassuring enough for ○ in the beginning. But, as time wore on, ○ began to wonder if she'd set herself up as the fool.

Her love became her focus as she sought to keep the frustration neatly bottled up inside. But that ache was an energy that had to be released in some form of thought or deed. The longer ○ denied the fact that her marriage to X was not meeting her needs for attention, the more lethal the situation became for her entire being.

This reoccurring theme in ○'s life—neglect—had haunted her from childhood to marriage. This was responsible for the pervasive unconscious fear that greeted ○ every day. With a brood of seven siblings, ○'s mother had been too busy to give ○ the attention she needed as a child, thus creating a series of irrational behavior patterns that plagued ○ still to this day. Insecurity, anger, and low self-esteem caused ○ a great deal of suffering whenever her "neglect" buttons got pushed. This was her greatest demon, and little did she realize her marriage was playing the same old tune. Until the neglect issue was resolved, it would follow her for the rest of her life. ○'s sense of self-worth would never fully be realized, no matter how well she pretended otherwise. Deep down she felt an impending doom.

"Damn that twitch! Where are my glasses?"

Denial: a comforting friend until it wears out its welcome.

It was early morning. The sound of X's boot heels fell softly on the bedroom floor. O woke, as she'd done two times during the night already, wondering when her lonely night would end and X would return to their bed. Sunbeams filtered in through the sheers. X silently slid into bed next to O, who was pretending to be asleep, his arm pulling her close to him. She lay motionless with a heavy heart. Sleep came to him quickly—her cue to slip out of bed.

There was plenty of time for O to hit the gym before X woke for their Sunday brunch ritual. She gathered her gym bag and jumped in the car. What she found on the floor of the car that morning, however, would have a profound effect on her life.

Don't jump to conclusions, O consoled herself as she reached down to pick up the crumpled pair of black fishnet stockings. *It can't be as bad as it seems. It just can't be!* Judging by their trampled appearance, X must have found them on the side of the road as he got out of the car, she thought. He and his friend V probably got a real good chuckle out of it. "Finders, weepers," whispered a voice in her head.

"The Moment You Believe" by Melanie C blasted from the radio as O took off in a flurry of uncertainty. "I'm ready now to start a new beginning …" O half wondered if the lyrics were trying to tell her something, but then she shrugged off the thought as it was far too painful to entertain, and she was not yet ready to listen.

O tried focusing on her workout and the magazine she held in front of her, which just happened to open directly to an article on sex—an apropos theme for her morning so far. Sex, so it claimed, was the gateway to a higher state of consciousness and the vehicle that joined both the physical and spiritual bodies. Through sex, it said, the oneness created between two people mirrors the oneness that exists between all things in the universe. That was a bit too far-fetched for O to grasp, though it gave her a good chuckle as she dismissed the ridiculous idea and tried to divert her attention to the television. The questionable history of the stockings, however, proved too heavy to ignore. *Too bad S is nowhere in sight,* she thought. He would have served as a much-needed distraction.

Filled with anxiety over the thought of confronting X with "the goods," O packed her gym bag and headed back home. How would this conversation end? she wondered.

"Good morning, Gem," greeted X, still looking half asleep as he intercepted ○ at the front door. "Have a good workout?"

"Oh, yes," responded ○, wondering how to introduce her found treasure. Maybe she should serve them for breakfast. "Uh, what's this?" she asked, holding up the pair of crumpled stockings.

"Uh, where'd you find these," he asked apprehensively.

"On the floor of the car," she responded in a flat, controlled voice that masked her pounding heart. X was silent for but a split second and then broke out in a fit of laughter.

"Ha! I can't believe it!" he cried out in surprise. "Last night V borrowed the car to pick up a girlfriend. Looks like they left something behind! I'll have to call that hound dog and make him apologize for causing you unnecessary worry, baby." Still chuckling, X wrapped his arms around ○ and kissed the top of her head.

○ was wavering in disbelief over X's reaction, which seemed far too smooth to be a lie. He might be good, but was he that good? She so wanted to believe him, because otherwise the implications were too threatening to her security and love for X to allow any thought of truth to his infidelity. Though ○ had always reserved in the back of her mind the idea that any man could be unfaithful in a marriage, even X, she truly believed in his commitment to her, and through the eyes of ○'s loving perspective his innocence prevailed.

○ accepted his explanation with hidden skepticism and denied herself any thoughts to the contrary. In an effort to put the event behind them, she went to the kitchen to start breakfast, rubbing her eye in defense of the annoying twitch that was flaring up again.

O was at her desk preparing for the executive director's meeting, which was in a couple of hours. She was nervous.

Hmm, how should I begin? "Good afternoon, gentlemen; how's it hanging?" *Nah, better not! Maybe something less provocative,* she chuckled to herself in an effort to keep her mood light and nerves in check.

O's position at Blush & Company as director of cosmetic innovations spanned eight years, quite a feat for a self-professed job-wanderer who had spent years in search of a final career destination. O, being an original personality, even exotic some would say, grew up feeling uninvited to the party. The director's position at Blush had finally given O the sense of confirmation and accomplishment she so longed for, allowing her the creative playground she needed to prosper. But this was not without conflict between her radical business ideals and those of the modern world. Her disdain for the excessive marketing tactics the beauty industry had developed in order to gain the attention of the consumer was difficult to ignore—they were tactics bordering on aggression and surviving on false claims.

O dreamed of becoming partner in the firm, now one of the leading cosmetic companies in North America. She'd brought them many successful and innovative product ideas. She'd been promoted three times in eight years and was ready for the next step. Her goal was to pave the way for a more sustainable future based on a new philosophy and business model, one that would incorporate corporate governance and responsibility as a primary objective. Her code of ethics supporting this endeavor would steer away from sensationalism exploited through empty product promises. Credibility in all of Blush's products would be founded on superior quality and actual results. The current marketing environment, unfortunately, was anything but that.

O believed strongly in work-life balance and putting an end to the ridiculous speed of doing business, driven by the greed for more, in which the average job translated into sixty- to eighty-hour workweeks. She wanted to put an end to the idea that holidays were merely a concept—God forbid an employee would dare take them literally. The competition to get ahead by working more, longer, faster eventually resulted in sick employees, both physically and mentally. The work environment had become toxic, and stress was the culprit. Burnout syndrome was epidemic. More frequently than ever, the newspapers were reporting on the use of brain-enhancing drugs being abused in the workplace to increase attention span and focus. This was slowly becoming the norm. Never mind the eventual side effects to one's overall state of health; it created a deadly competition among colleagues based on a work-till-you-drop philosophy. It was hard for O to fathom that this behavior was considered acceptable and was being exploited by the pharma industry through drug ads.

O felt trapped and disempowered by a corrupt system, a difficult fate for an idealist with ambition, but it also encouraged her to keep trying. Marketing had become the sole source of conspicuous consumption made to feed the ego and create an evil cycle of perpetual *wanting* in the public psyche. As a victim herself, she knew what she was talking about, and yes, this was not without shame for her own hypocritical participation. She was aware that once you were seduced by the system, it was difficult to shake the habit, let alone see it for what it was, which was the case for most of humanity.

The business model was the same everywhere in today's society: create new or improved products quickly before the public got bored; short-term goals brought quick cash;

worry about the future another time; grow, grow, grow. When did the growing stop? O questioned the logic. The market was so flooded with products that it had done nothing but create a dazed and confused public, numb from the in-your-face marketing strategy. Not to mention the impact consumption run amok had on the environment. Even at a very young age O concerned herself about such mundane things as trash and where it would all end up, a rather adult preoccupation for a six-year-old.

O knew customer loyalty couldn't be won when a beloved perfume suddenly disappeared from the market after a few short years because a *new* one had to be introduced, or a favorite lipstick color was dropped in order to introduce a new exciting color. *Is there even such a thing as a new color?* she asked herself. *Don't they realize how long it takes to find the perfect color in the first place? Who wants to do that every season!?*

O wasn't having fun in this self-serving game of greed. As a professional, she felt her life was at the mercy of everyone else. She had gotten lost playing a role and chasing the idea that having a secure job at a national corporation should suffice as a happy life. Blush had quadrupled the pace of production over the last five years. In truth, the margins weren't indicating that this philosophy was a good one. In fact, just the opposite was beginning to rear its ugly head.

Sooner or later, the truth would come to light. She knew it, but did anyone else? O vowed to change that one way or another.

O grabbed her notes, checked her look in the mirror, and made her way to the boardroom.

All the executive board members from A to Z, including the CEO, Mr. C, were present. Mr. G's team began with their presentation, and R got the ball rolling, followed by team members E and E, and rounded off by D. O now had the floor.

"Mr. C, I'm afraid I can no longer agree with the business model our company is practicing." O was either being very brave or very stupid. Her eight-year track record was long enough to win the respect of the others, but this approach might not go over too well.

"Do you mind explaining what it is you think would be the right business model, Mrs. O?" responded Mr. C with a twinge of sarcasm.

"The world is changing; people are evolving. We need to recognize this and react accordingly, responsibly, if we want to stay ahead of the game. The problem with the way business is conducted these days has a name—Greed. The singular goal carved out by the majority of businesses today revolves purely around money. Greed is running rampant in society. We need to rise above such shortsighted means of conduct and create a new corporate culture as a new business model for society at large. Protecting a public image that lacks any substance behind the-scenes is the sad reality for most businesses. Money has become the sole guiding factor in society's idea of success, and this is a grave mistake.

"Our focus needs to shift to the quality of our products and their value to our customers. Our actions should follow an ethical code of conduct that we define and which serves everyone's best interests internally, externally, and environmentally. This will create confidence that our products are superior to the competitors and will in turn build customer loyalty. Customer loyalty is what will lead to larger profits and is the reward and end result of such a strong work ethic. We're beginning to see the downfall now in our profit margins, as is the rest of the economy, due to the false philosophy that money is the center of the universe." ○ took a deep breath and a sip of water and continued.

"Money for the pure sake of money will sooner or later bring us down, gentlemen. Take the social media forums on the web as an example. Their popularity is increasing dramatically. People worldwide are publishing their grievances on these public forums. It's the wave of the future, which means people aren't just sitting back and accepting corruption anymore. The world is watching and keeping tabs. It's calling for transparency in all areas of life, from salaries to ethics, which are being graded against a newly emerging moral scale. Social media should become a standard part of our communication platform."

○ paused briefly to give her words time to sink in, ignoring a sudden wave of insecurity as she glanced around the room at the blank faces staring back at her.

"We have a choice: to be on the cutting edge of a new sustainable business model, one that supports our employees and rewards them on individual performance for their contributions to this company. Salaries and excessive bonuses should be in alignment with shareholders' opinions.

"We could take the initiative to form a partnership with an international environmental institution where we work hand in hand to provide financial support and help find solutions for sustainable business practices. This action will encourage others to follow suit and lock in consumers who support our cause.

"Work-life balance should take precedence over today's work-till-you-drop mentality. It's a fact that stress plays a vital role in the health of employees. Statistics show that over sixteen percent of workers rate their jobs as extremely stressful. Absenteeism translates into billions of lost dollars to the company and the healthcare system. This is where we can cut costs. Gifting our workers a balanced work environment with flexible work hours, a cap on overtime, courses on how to deal with stress, and activities to support their health is how we can save and contribute positively to the work experience for everyone at Blush. A happy employee is not only a healthy employee, but a more productive and motivated one. Healthy and motivated employees translate into increased profits.

"Additionally, we should take the local economy into consideration and balance our production forces. Producing exclusively overseas takes jobs away from our local economy, all so we can earn a higher profit. What happens next is exactly what we saw last year with Company Y. Their products produced in China were tainted with cancer-causing agents, and why was that? Because the Chinese have undercut themselves so much over the years that they've had to resort to cheaper, unethical manufacturing methods, forcing them to cut costs any way they see fit. There is a dark cloud on the horizon, gentlemen. Research shows customer brand loyalty has decreased by twenty-five percent. We won't be able to rely solely on our brand value in the future. We'll have to offer much more. People are tired of fluff at high prices. They want the real deal—substance." O paused while attempting to read the reactions of the others.

Mr. W, a distinguished gentleman with white hair and goatee, interjected. "Mrs. O, your comments are well noted. As you have proven yourself to be a trendsetter over the years, I'm confident your words will have a profound effect on our thoughts this evening. I, for one, appreciate you taking the risk to share your forward-thinking views."

"Indeed," grumbled Mr. C. "Let us adjourn for now. It's been a very productive meeting. Thank you all for your contributions today." He shot O a questionable glance before exiting the room. The rest of the board rose quietly like zombies and departed without comment.

○ let out a deep sigh of relief, glad that was now behind her. She wasn't sure how or if her words would be digested by the rest of the committee, but she knew she'd done something profound, for better or for worse. Either way, she had done what she'd been meaning to do for a long while. Was the fear beginning to subside or was insanity setting in, she wondered.

"Good work, ○. I'm proud of you," said Mr. W, patting her gently on the shoulder. "You're ahead of your time. Just be patient. Sleepwalkers don't wake easily."

○ was grateful for Mr. W's encouragement. He was a pillar of support for her, which gave her great comfort in times of need. They often sat together after hours and discussed themes of mutual interest, such as their involvement in environmental initiatives. Mr. W supported numerous environmental institutions and was on the board of Believe Foundation as one the leading pioneers in future solutions for a disintegrating world.

○ went back to her office and gathered her things. Her evening program consisted of a well-deserved bottle of red wine and a relaxing hot bath, the thought of which suddenly ignited an entirely different stream of thoughts; it didn't take much these days.

At home, ○ relaxed back into the sudsy wet warmth, wineglass in hand, piano music from Lang Lang in the background, and allowed herself to indulge in the world of her fantasies as the merciless itch beckoned for relief.

O was working at her desk when the phone rang. She could barely hear the voice on the other end.

"Hi, O, it's me," B whispered. "What are you doing in about an hour?"

"I'm free. Why, what's up?"

"A lot. The shit just hit the fan at the office today. I've got to talk to you. Can you meet me at the coffee shop on the corner in one hour?"

"Sure, B. See you there."

O had a bad feeling about this. There had been rumors lately about certain unethical practices in the pharma industry, and Medy had been fingered as one of the companies involved.

"O, I'm over here," B called out, waving her arm. She wore a fitted, low-cut ink blue dress that appeared to have been slept in and matching high heels, an ensemble color-coordinated with her eyes. A lengthy run was working its way up the stocking of her right leg.

"Thanks for coming on such short notice," B said in a tense voice.

"Of course. What on earth is going on, B?" O eyed her unruly appearance.

"You won't believe it. We were raided today at the office by the authorities. They confiscated our records and have cited us with an official warning against certain so-called unethical marketing practices," B explained, gasping for air.

"Whoa! Slow down and take a deep breath. You're starting to turn as blue as your dress," said O in an effort to calm her.

"You know, this is the last thing I need, like I'm not stressed enough," complained B. "We'll have to go to court on this. It could cost us millions! Shit, the papers are going to have a feast."

"Well, give me the details! What the hell is this all about, anyway?" pressed O.

"Where do I begin … I'll give you the highlights. We have a drug called KiL, passed by the FDA five years ago as a high blood pressure medication. It's been a real blockbuster for us. We're being accused by the authorities of marketing this drug for an additional unapproved purpose, against migraines. Some doctors have already been prescribing it to their patients. This is a big no-no in our business, O."

"Shit!" blurted O.

"You can say that again."

"Why would marketing take such a bloody risk? That's suicide!"

"Yeah …" B fell silent, diverting her eyes away from O's glare. "Heads are going to roll. I just hope to God mine isn't one of them."

"What do you mean? You didn't have anything to do with this, did you? Please tell me you didn't, B!"

B fumbled for words. "I've told you too much already, O. I really can't say more." Tears began to well up in her eyes. B gathered her things and got up to leave. She turned toward O. "Illusions. It's all about illusions. Those that fool us and those we use to fool others. Whatever happened to reality, O? Do we even know what that is anymore?"

B turned away to leave and then paused for one last thought. "Doesn't anybody care about people anymore? It's all about money isn't it, O? It's just one big game of money where humanity comes in last. Thanks for coming. I love you," she said as she turned and rushed out.

Though the real meaning behind B's comments was not yet clear to O, in time it would be.

It was disturbing to see B so distraught. B was always so full of life, so upbeat, even if it was to hide her proclivity to depression, which was her well-guarded secret. No one knew about it, not even O, for the longest time. She had only found out because B had inadvertently alluded to it over the phone when her guard was down. No wonder B had a tendency to disappear for weeks at a time without checking in. It had never occurred to O that B was hiding this dark truth about herself. B, who never hesitated to go out of her way to help others, particularly O, for whom she'd do anything, had a heart of gold. Unfortunately, B lived every moment of the past and future all at the same time. The present escaped her field of perception altogether. This unconscious mindset, no doubt B's effort to keep the depression at bay, served as its own poison that manufactured a constant state of stress and worry. It was self-medication through perpetual busyness—a disease many an unconscious soul engaged in.

As O exited the coffee shop, lost in thought, she bumped hard against what felt like a tree.

"Excuse me," said a male voice. "Oh, good afternoon, O! What a pleasant surprise!"

O gazed up into the deep blue eyes of Mr. S. Flustered, she dropped her bag on the ground, causing the two of them to smack heads as they both bent down for it.

"Sorry. Are you all right?" asked S.

"I'm fine, don't worry. I'm just a bit lost in thought at the moment and wasn't watching where I was going," O replied nervously.

S was dressed in a handsome dark gray business suit—quite a departure from his gym shorts but nonetheless exciting. Her heart raced. *Oh God, let me kiss those gorgeous lips of his just once in my life before I die,* thought O. She had an overwhelming urge to shake him by the collar and scream, "Fuck me already, would you!"

"Do you have a few minutes? I mean, if you're not in a hurry, we could have a quick coffee or something together," offered S.

The "or something" piqued her interest. O studied her watch in pretense. "Uh, well, sure! I suppose I could use a coffee. Haven't had one all day!" she lied.

"Well, we're in luck; I just live around the corner. We can go up to my place—that is, if you're not uncomfortable with that?"

Hmm, that's a good one, thought O. *Uncomfortable? Try delirious!*

O was hoping S couldn't hear the knocking of her knees as they walked in silence to his place. S opened the oversized brass-framed door to the building and led O to the small elevator. His closeness shot her blood pressure up faster than the elevator rose. The scent of his cologne awakened a sea of undiscovered emotions as it flooded her nostrils. She felt dizzy. *Oh God, give me strength,* she begged in the awkward silence. Excitement pricked the air. Every cell in her body was alive and pulsating. All her senses tingled as though awakened from a long sleep. Giggles accented O's words as she attempted to make small talk to ease her nerves. Just then the elevator halted with a jolt, allowing them to exit directly into his penthouse.

As O entered, her eyes darted around the room, taking in all the details. The air smelled like cherries. His apartment resembled a student's more than a banker's, she thought. The space was sparsely furnished and quite small, though it had a great view of the Mony River. *Separated or divorced?* she questioned herself silently. A man of his good looks at forty-something could never have escaped the grips of a beautiful woman. Of that O was certain. Besides, the gym towel edged in lace, which he often used, was a dead giveaway.

"I'm afraid I only have about fifteen minutes to visit, O. I have a meeting at one thirty," apologized S as he began to prepare the coffee.

That's enough time for a quickie, thought O. "No problem; I have to get back to the office anyway." O discreetly scanned the room in hopes of discovering more private details about the life of Mr. S. The space was rather sterile, very clean and orderly. She could see his bed from where she stood; it was dressed conservatively in solid tones of gray, black, and white. She imagined the kind of women he brought to his lair and the sort of dark secrets he must have stashed away in his closet. A basketball sat on the floor in the corner of the living room, but there were no personal photographs anywhere. Not exactly cozy. His place struck her as rather sad. Maybe it was the lack of warmth or personal details that were missing from the room, or the feeling of loneliness that permeated the air. O got the sense that he was somewhat of a loner. Whatever it was, she couldn't quite put her finger on it, but a sense of joy was definitely absent.

Then something odd happened. As if out of nowhere, O was overcome with emotion. She experienced an uncontrollable release of dammed-up tensions and without warning, burst into tears. "I'm so sorry; I don't know what's gotten into me! I've just got so much on my mind with work and personal issues." She fumbled around in her purse for a tissue as S magically appeared with one in hand. S, a bit stunned by this sudden development, approached O, gently putting his arms around her shoulders in an effort to comfort her.

"I feel so ridiculous! Forgive me for this silly outburst," O pleaded.

"Don't worry. I burst out in tears every once in a while myself," responded S.

Blinking through her tears as she studied him curiously for a moment, O realized he was just kidding in an attempt to lighten the mood. They both giggled.

"Sorry, I don't mean to poke fun at you," apologized S while handing O a coffee cup. They both threw back espressos in a fit of nervous energy.

"Listen, I need to get going, so why don't we exchange numbers and maybe we can get together sometime for dinner?" S suggested.

When? she thought. It couldn't be soon enough. That itch was begging for attention.

As night fell O was grateful, for once, for the time alone. X was out enjoying another nightly adventure with the boys. Occupied with thoughts of S, she finally fell into a deep sleep.

O woke suddenly at the sound of X stirring in the room. She peeked with one eye at the clock next to the bed. 5:00 am. Reeking of alcohol and cigarettes, X slid into bed beside her. He rolled over toward her, slid his cold hands beneath her nightgown, and cupped her small breasts. He began to kiss the back of her neck and shoulders. The smell of his clubbing clung to his skin and hair. It was enough to make her puke. He attempted to mount her ....

"Uck, you stink, honey! Can't you take a shower first?" pleaded O, holding him at arm's length.

"Never mind," mumbled X. "I'm too tired." He rolled over, said good night, and was fast asleep in seconds.

A heavy feeling washed over her. O's reaction could have permanent consequences on any hopes of a renewed sex life, not to mention their marriage. The D word flashed through her mind. O agonized over her impulsive reaction. What if this was it? She'd never forgive herself if their marriage came to an untimely end because of this one thoughtless moment. Her love for X, still very much alive, magnified her growing angst.

O yearned to take advantage of the crisp autumn day and managed to convince X to go on a hike with her. They were deep in the woods when X, holding his broken shoelace in his hand and looking quite annoyed, glanced over at O as if to say this would be the last time he'd ever agree to go on a hike with her again.

"Come on, X," encouraged O. "It's a beautiful day. The fresh air will do you good. How's your headache?"

"Fine."

"I'm sorry about last night, honey. I didn't mean it the way it came across," she apologized.

"I don't remember anything strange about last night. I was just very tired."

Hmm, O thought. She didn't really believe that. Maybe he was too drunk to remember, but she found that highly unlikely.

"Why are you so tense these days, honey? It's so unlike you to be agitated all the time. Is everything okay at the hospital?" X rarely shared the details of his job with her. He was masterful at turning it off as soon as he left the hospital.

"I received some disturbing news at work in the last few days," confessed X. "Did B say anything to you about an investigation?" he asked.

"Yeah, she did! Are you somehow involved with the Medy probe?"

"Could be, since I'm in close contact with the Medy reps. The investigators contacted me this week. They've been inquiring about corporate gifts, drug recommendations, etcetera. I don't know yet what this means for me, but let's hope I'm not nailed for malpractice."

"Good Lord! Is it that serious?" O became frightened. Not knowing enough about the implications, her imagination went wild.

"Don't start worrying about this, O. Just forget I mentioned it. We don't know anything concrete at the moment and can't do anything about it anyway, okay?" responded X curtly.

Don't worry? That was a foreign concept. It was worry that gave O the false sense of control that she could improve a situation or make it go away. She'd worry, all right. What else could she do, until she recognized worry's futile nature, but there were still lessons to be learned before that would happen. There was something else behind X's words, O sensed, that warranted its share of worry. He wasn't coming completely clean, thought O. These days he was preoccupied with something else besides work.

It was early the next morning. ○ was dressed and putting on her coat when her purse began to vibrate.

Who on earth would be sending me a message at this hour? she grumbled. She searched her bag for the phone, and there on the display was a message from Mr. S.

○ couldn't believe her eyes.

Good morning to you, ○. Wanted to know if you'd have time for dinner Friday evening. Let me know. Ciao, S.

Holly shit! What do I do? Can I really go through with this? ○'s mind was aflutter.

I don't know, I don't know ... I need some time to think. What if I say yes? What if I say no!? Will I get another chance? ○ felt sick to her stomach.

"Bye, honey," called ○, trying to keep her voice as natural as possible. She walked back to the bedroom where X was still in the midst of his morning routine.

"What'd you say, Gem?" he called, stepping out of the bathroom.

"I said bye; I'm leaving for the office. Oh dear, honey, you're bleeding. Did you cut yourself shaving?" she asked, noticing a long, thin scratch across his left cheek.

"No, my ring scratched me as I was washing my face. A piece of the wire detail broke off and left a sharp edge. So, don't be upset or worried if you don't see me wearing my wedding band for a while, okay? I'll have to send it in for repair before I can wear it again."

Symbols exist everywhere, pregnant with meaning to those open to their hidden messages.

Driving to work, O's stomach was nervous and upset. S's message came as a surprise. She hadn't expected to hear from him after the embarrassing episode in his apartment. Since then, she'd gone over and over the scenario in her mind. It was quite odd, this feeling she had when he hugged her. What was it? O searched for clarity. It was as though he was empty inside. She sensed no emotion from him, whatever that meant.

After arriving at the office, O sat down at her desk, took her phone in hand, and started to message:

Good morning, S. What a nice surprise to hear from you ... minutes went by, and then: *Yes, Friday is fine with me. Let me know when and where. Until then, O.*

Oh my God! I can't believe I'm going through with this. Let me just keep my big mouth shut. I don't need to tell a soul about this. It's just dinner anyway; good grief. I don't need to make more out of it than that, thought O trying to nip her rising guilt in the bud.

The problem was, that itch still needed to be scratched. O was desperate.

Guilt—a funny thing. It can stare you right in the face, and you'll deny its very existence.

O⁷

O had a standing lunch date every Thursday at noon with B at their favorite deli. O had already taken her place at the table. As usual, B was twenty minutes late, something O was getting used to. *Don't be a traitor*, she reminded herself about S. *B doesn't need to know about our dinner plans*. Just then the door to the restaurant flew open, and B scurried in, in an aura of chaos, cell phone to the ear. She looked tired and on edge.

"Oh, Lordy, it's hard to be old at such a young age!" she exclaimed, plopping herself down hard in the chair.

"Take it easy and take a deep breath; you'll be fine, B."

"What can I say … I'm planning on death by heart attack any minute now," B answered half-seriously. "On top of that, I feel like a schmuck because I went out with my new honey last night and fell asleep at his house and missed my morning coffee with J. He didn't appreciate that very much. Nevertheless, it was definitely worth the extra time at V's house last night. There's a good reason I'm tired today." Raising her eyebrows, B grinned and ran her fingers through her tousled hair as a bed feather came floating down and landed on the table in front of them, their eyes following it in silent pursuit.

"Well, I'm glad to see you have at least a couple of distractions. What's going on with the investigation?"

"I don't know if I'll survive this, O, and that's no joke. It's really not looking good. The authorities are accusing us of nondisclosure of vital test results from the trials of our KiL drug. It seems the Phase III trial results indicated possible life-threatening side effects of the drug, which were kept from the FDA. You know, O, so much money goes into researching new drugs like this one, that to lose FDA approval because of a *possible* side effect would have been devastating to our pipeline. We desperately needed this approval. I know that's no excuse when lives are at stake. I'm sure you understand what I want to say here."

"Quite frankly, B, I find it perfectly despicable. Whoever is responsible for this in your company should get a life sentence. I'm sorry, but I can't condone any such behavior, ever! Have you lost your sense of morality? I mean, maybe you're just too close to this and can't see the forest for the trees! Sometimes I don't think I know you at all." O was irritated. She felt somehow deceived by B. How could she be so happy-go-lucky with her sex life while simultaneously defending her company that was under investigation for the possible loss of innocent lives?

"Look, O, I know this sounds …"

O cut her off. "And, by the way, X has been summoned by the authorities for his involvement with your reps. This is really not funny anymore, B. I don't know how I'm supposed to feel about all this."

"Okay, girlfriend, just calm down and take a deep breath, all right? I don't need another casualty in my life. I need your support now more than ever. I don't think I'm going to make it through all this, O." Her voice quivered as she hid her teary eyes behind an unsteady hand.

"Don't worry, B. I'm not going to abandon you," O softened, reaching across the table to take B's hand. "I just want you to stop for a moment. Stop medicating yourself with meaningless sex and constant chaos. When was the last time you spent time alone and just enjoyed a good book and a home-cooked meal?"

"That's never happened," confided B, wiping at a tear that had escaped down her cheek.

"Speaking of books, I almost forgot." Reaching into her bag, B pulled out a large photography book and handed it to O.

"What's this?" she asked in surprise.

"Well, I was passing by the bookstore the other day and saw this in the window and immediately thought of you. It's full of gorgeous nature photos and universal wisdoms. It's right up your alley, isn't it?"

"Yes, yes. It's wonderful! Thank you so much, B." O leaned over the table and gave B a kiss on the cheek. "You're just too kind to me, you know that?"

"It's nothing. My pleasure, girlfriend."

"Anyway, getting back to where we were, B, you'll never find clarity the way you're living; you know that, don't you? Do you even know who you are anymore? You've gotten so lost in climbing the corporate ladder, lost in your own ego and ambition. I'm sorry if this is hard for you to hear, but I'm only saying this because I care about you, and I see what you're doing to yourself. You need to change the way you live, B, before you have a breakdown. Are you listening to me?"

"Yes, O, I'm listening, as always when you chide me about my lifestyle. I'm not you! I'd love to be quiet and home with my hubby on the couch watching movies, or sitting in bed every night reading self-help books, but I'm not you! I know I need to change. I know! I just don't know how." B jumped up, suddenly realizing time had gotten away from her. "Oh, shit! I'm late for a meeting. I'd completely forgotten! Thanks for hanging in there with me, O. I need lots of help, I know. I'll try to heed your advice. I will!"

Getting in touch with her inner being could be B's only saving grace, but then again, it might already be too late.

The path to healing lies at the seed of the hurt.

O was glad to finally be home; one more day, and then the weekend and dinner with S. She threw off her shoes and laid her purse down on the table in the foyer.

O picked up a silver key lying on the table next to her purse. *Hmm, what's this?* It didn't look familiar. O's left eye began that annoying twitch again. Just then her purse began to vibrate. Her heart skipped a beat. *Oh, God, is that S?* O frantically fished in her purse for her phone. It was indeed.

"*Hi, O. How's tomorrow night at 8:00 at Restaurant Temptations? Till then, S.*"

Okay. This is my last chance to bail. Hmm … O was indecisive. Just then the front door flew open. X landed in the doorway, giving O a shock of her life as her phone went flying out of her hands and a loud yelp escaped her lips.

"Sorry, Gem, didn't mean to scare you! What are you so jumpy about?"

"Nothing. I was just deep in thought about work and didn't expect you so soon, that's all." O's face went beet-red, as it did when she was lying. "Smooch?"

X obliged, placing a wet one on O's upturned lips. He hung up his coat and headed to the kitchen for a beer.

"X, what's this key for, here on the table?" asked O, rubbing her twitching eye. There was a pregnant pause. X's voice suddenly changed.

"Work. That's a key for work," he said in a strange, staccato-like manner. O knew that was a lie, but she couldn't for the life of her surmise why he would be lying about a key.

"O, I'm afraid I have a late meeting tomorrow evening and won't be home for dinner. So don't bother cooking for me, all right? Maybe we'll go out for a nice dinner on Saturday. What do you say?" X was doing his best to change the subject.

"Sure. That sounds nice. I'm going to get together with B tomorrow night anyway."

X seemed to stiffen at her comment. *Odd,* thought O, she but didn't think much about it. O now had an alibi and an open invitation to confirm with Mr. S. Even if she wanted to be good, the gate of opportunity had swung wide-open, daring her to walk through.

O⁸

Pulsating, aroused, a sense of rebirth and everything alive was the best way to describe O's physical and mental condition as she left the house for dinner with a growing appetite for Mr. S. The early fall weather was crisp and exhilarating, a good match to her state of excitement. There was a sense of newness in the autumn air as the days grew shorter and the leaves more colorful.

Her cheeks were hot and rosy from the endorphins streaming through her body. Even her lips were blushing, a complement to her indigo-colored blouse. What would happen? Would he try to kiss her? Would they just eat and say goodnight? Time would tell, and it was time that was killing her in trying to reach her destination. The restaurant was a ten-minute walk from the parking lot. She could feel the straps of her new garter belt pressing against her thighs as she walked. Each step of her black suede four-inch heels hitting the pavement echoed in her ears. Each step was an eternity. Anticipation masqueraded like deep mud against the will of a sex-starved forty-two-year-old woman—pure torture.

The restaurant, for better or worse, was very romantic, even sexy, with its black marbled bar, glossy black and white checkered floor, white leather upholstered booths, and Murano glass chandeliers, which cast soft shadows across the room. Yes, Temptations was a good choice; not too pricey and not too casual, although O's four-hundred-dollar shoes (a real bargain for making you feel like a million) were slightly over-the-top for the occasion. O couldn't care less.

O had paused in the entrance of the restaurant to look around for S when a sultry voice like the warm tone of a violin whispered in her ear from behind.

"You could get yourself arrested walking around looking that good."

O's heart skipped a beat as she spun around to find S standing there in all his glory, positively twinkling like she'd never seen him before. An unexpected feeling of insecurity came over her as she imagined all the women in the room as captivated by his sparkle as she was. A twinge of jealousy struck her surprisingly hard. He was simply too gorgeous to ignore.

"Good evening, S. Am I late? Have you been here long?" asked O nervously as she tried to steady her voice, adrenaline rushing through her veins.

"No, no, I only just arrived a few minutes ago. Here, let me help you with your coat."

The touch of his hands on her shoulders sent shock waves through her body. His hands brushed against the silk sleeve of her blouse, surely offering him some sense of erotic pleasure—a good start to the evening, she thought.

All eyes were on them as they followed the hostess to their private booth. Even perfect strangers could not ignore the powerful synergy between them. It connected them like an invisible cord. The residue of their synergy was almost palpable as it wafted through the air like a transparent film and lingered for the pleasure of the other dinner guests sitting in their wake. The element of danger kept ○ on edge, because no matter what role she played tonight, the voice of reason was always there reminding her who she really was: a married woman, who loved her husband, suffering from neglect, and desperate to have her itch scratched.

The two of them indulged themselves in the experience of one another as they savored every second, and what a spectacle they were to behold! The flirting, the giggling, the teasing, and the subtle sexual innuendos in their conversation were simply more fun than one could stand. Everyone present would have gladly traded places for but a moment of their shared pleasure. Applause was certainly due them for their entertainment, and had it been appropriate, surely the other guests would have obliged. The food and wine filled their senses, and as the night wore on they slowly migrated closer to one another. Whenever the moment allowed, their arms *accidentally* grazed each other's, greeting them with electric sensations. *This* is being alive, thought ○. *This is how life should feel every day. But, alas, such moments are fleeting.*

"Tell me what it is you do exactly, S. I know you work for your family's bank, but what is your game?" asked ○ playfully. By now she was more than slightly tipsy.

"My game? Well, I don't know about that, but I'm an advisor to the filthy rich, if that's what you want to know. Or, better yet, maybe you'd like to hear that I'm filthy rich?" he teased.

"Are you?" asked ○ in jest. "Don't answer that. Too much information will spoil all the fun, but it can't be easy these days to be a banker. Your reputation has been severely tarnished by this financial crisis. What do you have to say about that?" she asked, taunting him on.

"True, the environment has changed radically." S became introspective and quiet. ○ sensed that was perhaps not the best course of conversation, unless she wanted to find herself home alone this evening. Changing the subject was the best strategy.

"Let's delve into something sinful, shall we?" S offered instead, leaving plenty of room for misinterpretations.

The looming question of the evening was soon answered over a rich chocolaty soufflé. As O took a bite of its luscious liquid center a small portion of it dripped onto her bottom lip. S did not disappoint—before she could lick it away he scooped up her lips in his and sucked every last drop of chocolate clean from her mouth. Their lips lingered in the delicious sensation. Time seemed to stop. The moment melted into a long, dizzying kiss, igniting the flame of desire between them that had been simmering all night. They realized they had better leave the restaurant before they became the subject of a voyeur's dream. O's entire body tingled with excitement as the sensation of danger lurked in the air. A feeling of foreboding suddenly came over her. Brushing any negative thoughts to the back of her mind, she cast her cares aside. Tonight she was alive and wanted to live every single second of it. The only time that existed was now. There was no past, and there was no future. In this moment, she played the role of another woman—one who had nothing to lose.

"Might I entice you to my place for a private viewing of my ... *butterfly* collection?" questioned S, hoping for a positive response.

"Oh ... *butterf*lies?" questioned O with a silent hiccup. Measuring his cleverness, O responded, "Absolutely. I love them already!"

"Well, in that case, let's skip that part and move on to something more ... stimulating." They both giggled, knowing full well the direction the evening was about to take.

The instant the elevator doors closed, S wasted no time. He couldn't resist O any longer. He came to her, putting his arms tightly around her waist and pressing his body hard against hers. She succumbed willingly and longingly to his advances with full abandon.

"O, you move me," breathed S in a soft buttery voice while stroking her long silky red hair.

Hungry kisses starving for more, breathless whispers and electric sensations exchanging like rapid fire between their two bodies set the night in motion as they rode the elevator to the top. It's a wonder they survived, literally falling out of it as it landed with a jolt in S's penthouse.

A steamy story of fulfilled yearnings and unbridled passions occupied the hours that followed. Suffice it to say—O's itch finally got scratched. Hallelujah!

A fool's world parading as heaven can be blinding in the heat of passion.

It was one o'clock in the morning when O unlocked her front door and stumbled back into reality. There was no danger of X arriving home anytime soon. Alone time—that was what she needed; time for her thoughts, time to sort out her feelings. She reflected on what she had learned about S over the course of the evening, although more important things than chatting were on their agenda.

Between the flirting and the wine, S had reluctantly revealed a bit more of himself as his defenses gave way, seeming somewhat apprehensive to discuss too much of his private life.

S had grown up in Home with an older brother, an overbearing, image-conscious mother, and a workaholic father. He and his brother had become estranged from one another in recent years. The largest bank in the area was founded by S's great-grandfather and passed down through the family. After S's father inherited the bank, he expanded it into several other branches. S gradually took on more and more responsibility, as much as his father allowed. He also served in various chair positions in a variety of influential social clubs, to please his mother, who ultimately was responsible for his arranged "socially correct" marriage of ten unsuccessful years. With a failed marriage behind him, his mother had certainly left her mark, but it was S's need to live up to and beyond his father's expectations that drove him. He spent his lifetime seeking his father's love and approval, O surmised. Sadly, his dad had passed away some years ago, leaving S with an empty opponent's seat to compete with. The fact that his older brother now wore his father's shoes put stress on their brotherly relationship. That was bound to leave a lasting scar on S's life in some way. How exactly, O wasn't sure yet. But she did know one thing about S: image was everything, and he'd go to great lengths to protect it.

O could still smell S on her skin as her thoughts switched back to the more tantalizing events of the evening. What had she just done? It was one of the most exciting nights of her life. It was her reward for living this sex-starved existence of hers. Though she allowed herself this indulgence, guilt was no friend. That aside, it seemed like the best of both worlds: a husband she loved on the one hand and a passionate lover on the other … unless of course, she was to fall in love with the lover, a cardinal sin against one's own heart. What then? Did she love S? She began to see the possibility of loving two different men at the same time. But was he the one she'd always dreamed of? It felt that way, adding complexity and agony to her mounting confusion. Such deep-seated questions have led many into the dungeons of hell.

When O awoke, X was sound asleep next to her. She hadn't heard him come in. O slipped quietly out of bed and put on her sweats and running shoes, stopping briefly to observe him sleeping.

How could I do such a thing to X? O agonized silently. *I love him so much. One time is forgivable, isn't it? He would never do that to me.* O's guilt in the stark morning light brought a harsh reality to the disintegrating thrill of the night before.

O left the house at a fast jog—remorse tagged along. Avoiding the gym would be her tactic, at least for now. As she ran, she played the evening with S over and over again in her mind.

Physically she felt reborn. S had rescued her from sexual suicide—a ceaseless, agonizing ache, like a slow death of the soul, brought on by denial of one's own natural yearnings. O had never imagined that a woman's body could be so desperately in need of sex. She'd always believed that was solely a man's territory. O had denied her body for so long she'd become numb to its cry. Her soul suffered the toll. She was now beginning to get an inkling of the truth behind the article in the magazine she'd read days ago in the gym. Perhaps, indeed, there was a much deeper truth to sex than the obvious physical pleasure alone.

Returning home after her run, O showered and started breakfast. Over the sizzling sound of the frying eggs she barely heard the audible sound of her phone pleading for attention from the depths of her purse. It was a message from S:

Dear O, thank you for a very special evening. When can I see and touch you again? Kisses, S.

O was suddenly overcome by a gut-wrenching urge to throw up. Not exactly the reaction she had anticipated. The weight of her actions suddenly hit hard. Fear of being found out rushed in, and her thoughts became irrational—surprising considering her decision and pleasure to allow S's seduction. The moment the control of the pursuit fell into S's hands was the moment O perceived the potential for dangerous consequences.

"Oh shit, what have I done? He wants more! I didn't expect him to want more. It was just this one time. I don't really even know S that well. What if he pursues me and this turns into a fatal attraction? He can't pursue me; I'm married! I mustn't let this happen again. This'll have to be the first and last time," O promised herself.

O⁹

It was still dark outside when O arrived at her office and turned on the light. Mondays were not her favorite days of the week, particularly in the dark. It was earlier than usual; she couldn't sleep. Her stomach was in knots. Work was a good outlet in which to invest the energy.

50

O picked up the yellow note stuck to her computer screen:

O, please come to my office when you get in. Thanks, Mr. W.

Nothing to worry about, she told herself, unconvinced. Even though O shared a special closeness with Mr. W, who had served as a mentor to her over the years, she had had a feeling of uneasiness since her presentation to the board. Regardless, she was compelled to speak out about the very things that plagued not only today's global business structure, but also society at large. She'd stand by her convictions, if anyone needed further convincing, but perhaps it was O herself who needed reassurance of her stance, as she mentally recapped her position in the world.

O's vision of the future was so diverse from others that she continually felt misunderstood. Pessimists saw her as a dreamer and optimists as an idealist. She preferred the word *visionary*, but then everything was relative in the world. She saw war for what it was—primitive—and politics as nothing but a game big people play, all of which served to control the population, divide the world, and perpetuate suffering.

O's innate ability to think outside the box allowed her to see beyond society's current limitations. She envisioned a new moral standard for mankind where every individual took responsibility for the whole and where service to society was their primary goal. Unfortunately, most couldn't see beyond their own self-serving policies, their egos, and their desires for never-ending growth and consumption.

What O longed for was perhaps not possible within the minds of man in today's society. Humanity blindly suffered, and perhaps rightly so. What better way to learn than through experience? Such a radical shift was needed for her vision to be realized that it seemed hopeless to even entertain it. Yet she did. Somehow, some way, she would bring a new perspective forward in the world, even if it took her the rest of her life. This mission, along with her environmental concerns and efforts to find sustainable solutions, was such an integral part of O's being that it could not be ignored. O was driven toward something greater she had yet to discover in herself. It was a yearning, with neither a path nor a definition, that would one day take over and show her a new life's journey. But that time was still in the making.

O still had a couple of hours before Mr. W got in the office. She was under pressure to finalize her new product launch and had to refocus her attention on an idea she'd been working on for some time: an eyebrow enhancer never before seen on the market. It was as revolutionary as the curling mascara of years ago. This would surely redeem her in the eyes of the board, she thought, as the anticipated reward of success would satisfy their thirst for more (money). Though ○ loved creating innovative products and discovering new sustainable packaging methods, her heart was in direct conflict with the mandate to constantly produce and flood the market with new products, feeding the epidemic of conspicuous consumption. ○ was drowning in the very system she condemned. Becoming partner and implementing her own business strategy was the only way to be able to get up every morning and look herself in the mirror. Her chances of surviving in a job as a self-professed hypocrite were otherwise marginal, as she suffered from a lack of self-esteem to begin with.

Integrity is to kings as lies are to traders.

O was preparing to leave for Mr. W's office when her phone rang.

"O speaking."

"Hi, darling, it's me, B."

"B! You don't sound too good. Do you have a cold?"

"No, no, I had a late night. Fun, but late." O could only imagine what that meant. "O, I need to speak to you as soon as possible. Can you meet me for a drink after work today?"

"Uh, I think so. Let me just check my calendar." Mondays were her usual night at the gym, but under the circumstances a good excuse not to go was welcomed. "Yeah, it looks good."

"Okay. How about if we meet at seven at SeKrets?"

"Sounds good. See you then, B. And hey, don't worry so much. I hear it in your voice. Everything will work out. Life has its own agenda sometimes—you know what I mean? There's a reason for everything."

"Right, O. I hope you remember that advice this evening," responded B flatly. "Ciao."

Hmm, odd, she thought.

O looked at her watch and hoped she was not too late for her visit with Mr. W as she hurried down the hall to his office.

"Good morning, Mr. W," greeted O.

"Ah, yes, good morning, my dear. I see you got my note; very good," Mr. W said with a smile. "Come in and take a seat. Could I offer you a coffee or tea?"

"Yes, thank you. A tea would be great."

O took a seat next to Mr. W on the black leather couch, curious about what he wanted to discuss. He took his time to organize his thoughts before proceeding.

"O, I've been thinking over your presentation the other day at the board meeting," started Mr. W. "You were very brave, I must say. Your comments were dead-on."

"Thank you, Mr. W, for saying so."

He continued. "Using the word *greed* in the chairman's presence, however, was a rather risky choice," he said with a chuckle. "The reaction in his eyes was priceless! We all know very well his stance on bonuses, and that's to say nothing of his salary. He is the epitome of the false business model you spoke of. Perhaps that's even his life's purpose. That rather makes him the fall guy, now, doesn't it?" he quipped.

"The fact is, the entire planet is in a crisis, O, just as you've indicated in your presentation. Perhaps the greatest one mankind has ever seen, and we are only at the tip of the iceberg. There are systems and theologies in place that no longer serve mankind. Greed and ego will be our downfall." Mr. W paused to take a sip of coffee. "O, I'm an old man. I'm facing retirement and will no longer have an influence here at Blush & Company. I've been here fifty years! I gave it my best. Made it my life's work. What I'm trying to say is, don't waste your life as I have."

O was suddenly taken aback. She hadn't anticipated this direction in the conversation.

"This company has contributed to the greed of society, to the greed of the stockholders, and supported every person in upper management who earned money by unethical means, which I won't get into." He cleared his throat and continued. "I've been a part of this system, O. I'm willing to admit my failures, and I'm ashamed of my participation, because all the while I was too caught up in the system's false rewards to do anything against it. O, I feel I've lost the opportunity to create a better way, a more ethical way. Fifty years of my life are gone, and I have little to be proud of. I was greedy, just like the rest of them. "

"But, Mr. W …" interrupted O. "I …"

"Let me please finish, O," he said clearing his throat again. "Until the shareholders, the employees, and management, and I'm referring to all corporations worldwide, begin to regulate and overhaul the current system by which our leaders' salaries are determined and the ethics by which companies operate, the world's economy will suffer, our social system will become more and more dysfunctional, and deserving individuals will struggle a never-ending battle for justice."

"Mr. W, of course, as you know I'm in complete agreement, but about your contribution to this company, aren't you being a bit hard on yourself? You've done a great deal to bring this company to success."

"Believe me, O; things have gone down in this company for the pure sake of profit. Even as greed stared us straight in the face we ignored our despicable behavior."

O was speechless. She hadn't anticipated such a confession by Mr. W.

"O, the reason I asked you here this morning is to save you from making the same grave error I did. Follow your heart. Do what you know to be a positive contribution to your life and to others. Seek that which you can give back to the world. Put your ideas and talents toward changing this world for the better, because from here on out, we all need to make different choices. Our society as we know it is collapsing. Humanity is at the brink of a new era, which needs leaders like you. Step up to the plate, O. Don't waste your chance to be a part of this important change."

Mr. W sat down heavily in his chair. There was a state of calm around him, as though a huge weight had been lifted from his shoulders. He seemed deeply tired.

"O, there's one more thing." Mr. W drew in a somber breath. "I'll, uh … be leaving sooner than expected. I regret to have to tell you this, but I'm … dying of cancer. I've been under therapy for a few months but with little progress. We now need to take a more aggressive approach. I can no longer deny the inevitable."

The news hit O like a sledgehammer. It took her several moments to fully absorb his words. She began to lose her composure as tears welled up in her eyes. In reflection, O realized he'd been absent an unusual amount over the last few months and hadn't looked well for a long time. Why hadn't she been paying closer attention, she chided herself.

"Oh, dear God, please tell me that's not true, Mr. W. I can't bear to hear that."

"I'm afraid it is true, my dear. I'll be going in the hospital tomorrow. The cancer is too advanced," he explained.

"You've been one of the most important people in my career here. You've supported me in all my crazy ideas and in all my failures. I wouldn't have made it this far without you." O began to cry.

"Come, come now," comforted Mr. W. "Please don't shed any tears for me. I'm just another false hero like so many of us in the world today. But at least I'm lucky enough to live it out anonymously, unlike public figures—prisoners of their own celebrity—who must lose face before the public's eyes. All the false heroes of the world will slowly reveal themselves as undeserving creatures through their own demise, sooner or later. Such are the times we now face."

O was baffled by his comments. "You shouldn't say such things, Mr. W. You'll always be my hero," she said like a child to a parent. Mr. W was her King Arthur, as she'd shared with him in the past, a dashingly handsome charmer possessing manners of a bygone era, a real knight in shining armor in O's view.

"O, there's something else you should know. I know this will be painful for you to hear, but I think it's important that you know this about me. I'm no King Arthur, I can assure you. I've participated in what one might call *indiscretions* over the years. O sat rigidly in silence, waiting with bated breath for what was to follow.

"Many years ago I met a woman. She was the daughter to the CEO of one of our greatest competitors. He's someone I never took a liking to. He was a despicable man. Anyway, she and I shared the same feelings toward her father. I fell madly in love with this woman. It was a love affair that spanned nearly nine years. She was unhappily married to one of the executives of the company with whom she had three children. I loved this woman dearly, O, and would've done anything to hold on to her."

O blinked hard as she tried to consume the shocking words of Mr. W's confession.

"During the span of our affair she provided me with information on new products and ingredients her father's company was developing. Secrets that would be devastating if a competitor were to find out about them. Indeed. I used those secrets to our own advantage. But as her father's company began to falter, her conscience got the best of her. She could no longer continue her deceit to her family and tried to break off all contact with me. I was furious and broken. I couldn't imagine life without her. In an irrational moment I threatened to expose her, ruining every part of her life and reputation, if she left me. I can't be sure, but I believe it was the stress of my threat to her that led to her demise. She began having episodes of confusion and hallucinations, which gradually increased in frequency. She was diagnosed with schizophrenia and eventually institutionalized. My own selfish needs destroyed the love of my life, not to mention the agony it caused all those who loved her too. I will never forgive myself, and now as I face my own pending death, O, and at the risk of losing your love, I couldn't go to my grave without confessing that to someone I care about. I know my actions will be very difficult for you to accept and understand. I'm not proud. If there's anything to be learned from this, O, just know that the power of love is an uncompromising thing—when used for its own sake love can conquer all, but when used as a weapon it cannot endure. Irreparable damage to the heart and soul is forever."

There was a palpable quiet in the room. O sat silent for what seemed like an eternity to them both. Too stunned to say more, O rose quietly from her seat, nodded in slow motion to Mr. W as if departing the presence of a king, and replied, "I'm sorry to hear that, sir." She turned as though in a daze and made her way back down the corridor to her office.

O spent the rest of the day in silence, alone in her office trying to sort out her feelings, her mood somber. Hopefully the evening with B would offer some degree of comfort and distraction. Focusing on her work, O looked forward to the day's end.

B paced back and forth outside the restaurant with her cell phone to her ear, smoking a cigarette. The wind had a steely bite to it. The inner lining of her leather pants was strangling her right upper thigh with each step. Her feet ached from the stiletto heels of her fourteen-hour day. The time had come for B to reveal to O the truth about her dirty deeds.

"B, B, I'm here," called O in the distance as she approached, running. "Sorry to keep you waiting."

"Dammit, O, where've you been?" blurted B impatiently. "Gee, you don't look so good, girlfriend, what's up?"

"I got bad news at work today, but I don't really want to go into it right now or I just might lose it!"

"Great," said B under her breath. "You're really going to love this conversation." O flashed her a puzzled look.

"Come on, let's go in; it's chilly out here." B opened the door for O and followed in behind her.

The hostess led them to a quiet table in the back corner, exactly as B had instructed.

"What do you say we start with a couple of cosmos to forget about the events of the day?" suggested B.

"Sounds good to me," agreed O. The waitress took their order and soon returned with two pink cocktails.

The two of them made small talk over dinner, avoiding the more serious matters of the world before diving into the real meat of the evening. A good meal between friends—a simple pleasure so often overlooked for its real-life contribution to happiness. After two more pink ones they were primed for an enlightening conversation.

"So, getting down to more pressing matters," began O. "What's been going on with the case at work?"

"It's grave, O. In fact, the reason I invited you to dinner tonight was to tell you a couple of things, which are not going to be very pleasant for you to hear."

O fell silent, listening intently to what B was about to reveal.

"Before I begin, I want you to know that you are one of the best friends I've ever had. You mean so much to me I can't bear the thought of losing your friendship."

"You're not going to lose my friendship, B; what are you talking about?" asked O, miffed.

"O, I haven't been honest about a few things regarding my role at work. There's also, uh … a private matter I have to come clean with."

"Oh, shit. I think I'm going to be sick," warned O.

B sat back and drew in a deep breath as though preparing for an upcoming battle. "About two years ago, I had an affair with the corporate head of our division, a.k.a. *Dick Wad*; 'scuse my French. Anyway, during this affair he shared some information with me about the KiL drug I mentioned to you before. Remember? It had just completed the Phase III trials. Unfortunately, the researchers discovered some potentially lethal news at the last minute that would prevent the FDA from approving it. We couldn't let this happen. We were already suffering a loss in our second and third quarters, and there was lots of pressure from the shareholders to produce. Apparently, there were questionable side effects of the drug, and if injected improperly it could lead to serious consequences, but the chances were remote that anyone would ever die from this. For this reason, we (or he, DW) thought it was worth the risk to cover up the damaging evidence. I, at the time, blatantly refused, O! I hope you believe that."

"I'm listening; go on," replied O stiffly, arms folded across her chest.

"He wanted me to handle the marketing of the drug, prepare the brand kits for the sales reps, and push the drug hard. On top of that, he later saw an opportunity to position the drug for another use as well, to get more bang for the buck, so to speak. Well, I objected to this whole scheme, but he was very persuasive. I was in love with him, which made the matter that much more confusing for me. He promised me a kickback from the sales, if the drug made it to the market, and a promotion for the job I had my eye on, but the money didn't mean anything to me. When I refused to go along with his plan, O, he threatened to blackmail me by using our affair against me."

B was clearly at the end of her rope. The weight of bearing that dirty little secret showed in every line on her face. She let out a long sigh of relief. Show and tell had its rewards.

O was silent. Dumbfounded. Angry. Disappointed. Shocked.

"I really wish you would say something, O. Your silence is killing me!"

"So what's with the case, then? How do you rank in the scheme of things?" O questioned coldly.

"I'm in big trouble, O. If the authorities follow the trail back to me I could be tried for nondisclosure with intent to fraud, false advertising, marketing a drug for an unapproved purpose, and, last but not least, murder. There have been several deaths in connection to the side effects of the drug. What a bloody fool I was."

"I—I honestly don't know what to say, B," replied O coldly. How could this woman sitting before her, her best friend, do such a thing? How could O ever forgive her? How could she have not sensed something wrong? O felt totally deceived.

"What else did you want to tell me, B? Might as well get it all out in the open."

"I saw you the other night at dinner with S," B blurted out. O stopped breathing.

"*What?!* You saw me?" she cried in shock, suddenly remembering that feeling of uneasiness that had come over her, which she had chosen to ignore. "Where were you?"

"I was walking by outside and just happened to glance in through the window. I must say, I couldn't quite believe my eyes, but there you were with Mr. Sexy having a good laugh and flirting up a storm."

O was silent, not sure what all this meant yet. Was she going to blackmail her for some reason? Use this as ammunition for something she wanted? O's thoughts were spinning out of control.

"Now, here's the part you're really going to love—I was with X," said B bluntly.

"X? As in my X?" questioned O, bemused.

"Yes, as in your X."

What does that mean? What does she mean? O questioned herself in desperate search for an answer.

"Baby, do you remember the fishnet stockings? Do you remember the key on the entrance table you found? Those belonged to me. They're mine," confessed B.

"What are you telling me? I don't understand." O's mind was spinning. *Could this be true? What the hell is going on?* "Am I in the wrong movie?" cried O, hands pressed to her head.

"I'm so, so very sorry, O. But it's over between us. It's over!"

"Gee, that's comforting," snipped O.

"This is where your husband figures into the drug case. DW convinced me that if I could hook up with an influential doctor it would put us on the right course. I had met X a few times to inform him about the drug. It was strictly business, you understand. I figured I had a better chance of getting him to prescribe the drug for an additional purpose than our reps would, since he and I already knew each other. Then one thing led to another. We felt very comfortable with one another. Being that you're my best friend and all, it was so familiar. We had no agenda. But without any intention we let our affections slip beyond the line of friendship. There were never any serious feelings between us, O." B paused to let her words sink in.

"You don't need to worry about X. He did not see you with S that night, and I didn't say anything to him. O, he loves you, not me. He's told me that on numerous occasions. I know that one hundred percent. I was nothing but a distraction for him. It meant nothing. Really!"

O became unusually calm. What could she say? She, herself, was having an affair! That made her no different from X or B. How could she possibly be angry? How could she call the kettle black? It was almost funny. O began to giggle, which rapidly blossomed into uncontrollable laughter. B couldn't resist and joined in. The two of them sat at their table hysterically laughing, crying, and suffering together, in truth and in friendship.

O's head landed like dead weight on the pillow. She was drunk, emotionally drained, her mind a whirl of confusion … too tired to think anymore.

Darkness fell.

Morning came all too soon. The alarm rang for several minutes before O could muster the strength to turn it off. Friday morning. One more day before she could bury her thoughts in the idea of a weekend. Suddenly, it dawned on her. On the night of her dinner with S, she had told X she was going out with B! He was with B that night. Her alibi was shot clear out of the water. Of course, to say anything would be giving himself away. O glanced over at the sleeping X. He was stone still after coping with an emergency in the middle of the night. What did he make of her lie? O's stomach burned.

Uncertainty and fear of the unknown, all things that truly weigh on a person's psyche, were bearing down on O. *How does one filled with so much anxiety move without being paralyzed by it all?* she asked herself.

$\bigcirc$10

O had just come into the office when her cell phone rang. It was S. She gasped as she fumbled with the phone, not knowing whether to take the call or not, but the ring was painfully persistent.

"Hello?" she finally answered in a tentative voice.

"Hi, stranger! Haven't heard from you. Are you hiding from me?" questioned S half-seriously.

"Hi, S. No, no, of course not," she lied, unconsciously twisting her wedding ring around her finger. "I've just been somewhat overwhelmed with life lately, that's all."

"Well, I hope it's nothing serious." Without waiting for a reply S continued. "Will you be at the gym tonight? It'd be great to see you."

His voice had an undeniable power over her. O burned for him all over again. "Yes, I'll be there, probably around seven o'clock," she replied in spite of herself.

"Great! See you then."

"I'm weak. I admit it," she confessed out loud. *I've got to set my eyes on him and those gorgeous shoulders one more time.*

Escape came easily when the opportunity presented itself. The butterflies were already fluttering in anticipation. As she glanced down at her hand, ○ suddenly remembered feeling something rough on her ring while on the phone. As she looked more closely she discovered that a small piece of decorative wire that rimmed the edge of the band had broken off, leaving a sharp edge. *How very bizarre*, she thought—both their wedding bands had broken. First X's ring and now hers! Though luckily for ○, she escaped the scratch across the face.

Broken rings, broken vows—the message from the universe spoke loud and clear about the state of her marriage, but ○'s denial was deafening.

The face of truth has many guises.

The only way for O to make it through the rest of the day was to bury herself in her work. The new eyebrow enhancer with built-in wax that defined every brow hair with color and lasting shape would be the next revolutionary product for Blush & Company. O would be presenting to the marketing team in the coming weeks.

O noticed the red light blinking on her office phone when she returned to her desk with a cup of tea in hand. X's number read on the display. *Oh dear, what could that be about?* she wondered. Anxiety stirred as she dialed him back.

"Hi, sweetie," greeted O in a false voice. "Did you call?"

"Hi, Gem, yeah, I thought you might like to watch a movie tonight and order some pizza. Didn't know if you'd already made plans with B or not. So I'm making an official date with my wife!" It was a thoughtful measure by X, if not out of character. He had such an irresistible endearing quality about him. O was a sucker for it every time. She loved him in spite of everything.

"Aha, I see," said O, rubbing her eye as it began to twitch again. "Well, that's awfully nice of you, honey! I was planning on going to the gym, but we can do that afterward, okay?" responded O, glad not to have to lie in order to steal a moment with S.

"Sounds good. I won't be home till eight thirty probably anyway. See you then, love."

O's nerves were on edge. Was it really as innocent as all that or did X have ulterior motives? Uncertainty flooded her mind. In light of his affair with B, she didn't know how to act or what to say. She decided, after much deliberation, to take it as it came. No plans. No confessions.

Upon arrival at the gym, O scanned the room for S. No sign of him yet. She went to the locker room to change.

O mounted the step climber while glancing in the direction of the free weights, but still no sign of S. *Perhaps he changed his mind and isn't coming,* she thought. Her heart sank at the thought. At least her eye had stopped twitching. Just then she spotted S coming out of the locker room. Their eyes locked on one another. He looked at O with the kind of look that hits a woman right in the pit of the stomach.

"Hey, gorgeous; nice to see you again in the flesh!" Oh, if he only knew the thoughts sparked by that comment.

"Great to see you too, S," responded O almost bashfully.

"What do you say we catch a drink together after the workout?"

"Well, I don't have much time this evening, S, but perhaps next week sometime," offered O as a consolation. *But wait*, she thought, *what the hell am I thinking?* She was just setting herself up again. She knew she couldn't resist S. The attraction was too powerful.

"Now, that's a possibility," responded S with a wink. "I'll talk to you later. Gotta hit the weights." S was off to work on keeping his hard body hard. O picked up the tempo on her step climber in hopes of warding off the growing wave of sexual tension.

O had showered and was handing back her locker key at reception when S approached from behind, his cologne stirring an emotional wave of desire.

"So, Miss O, may I have the pleasure of escorting you to your car?" offered S.

"Why yes indeed, sir, that would be my pleasure," responded O in her best faux Southern accent.

They walked silently together, taking the stairs down to the garage. There was no one else to be seen as S pulled O aside into a secluded corner.

"O, you've been weighing seriously on my mind," breathed S heavily as he slid his hand firmly around the small of her back and pulled her near. "I have to see you again ... touch you, feel you," he whispered in her ear while pulling her closer still.

O's entire body awakened. *Help me*, she cried to herself, her heart pounding in her ears. *How do I resist this man?*

S's restraint had reached its limit. His hungry lips impatiently captured O's. A shared moment of lust needed no further encouragement.

"God, you drive me wild, you know that?" S moaned with a breathless voice. "I could take you right here, right now!" he threatened.

O was on fire. Her mind was blurry. She couldn't think straight. *Just touch me*, she thought. *Just touch me and you'll know I'm ready to be taken.*

"Stop. Stop," said ○ abruptly, breaking the tension. "I can't! It's the hardest thing in the world for me to say right now, but not here. Not like this."

"Okay, okay; that's fine." Though S was disappointed, not to mention in pain, his appetite for ○ would simply have to wait.

○ drove home in a daze. The affair with S proved to be a double-edged sword—both exhilarating and disturbing. It remained a source of confusion and fear, rendering her helpless in bringing it to an end, at least not yet. S filled the void, scratched the pervasive itch. Unfortunately, the physical toll on ○ was mounting—stomachaches, IBS. A sure sign something was amiss in her life. Where was her life heading?

X was pulling out the dinner plates from the cupboard for the pizza and movie night when ○ arrived home.

"Hi, love, I'm home," announced ○ as she opened the front door. "I smell pizza! Oh, what's this?" A single red rose stood in a vase on the entry table. ○ sniffed its soft scent.

"Can't a husband give his wife a rose without raising suspicion?" responded X somewhat defensively as he peeked his head around the kitchen corner.

"Well, of course. That's so sweet, honey. Thank you!" she said, putting her suspicious thoughts aside.

X greeted ○ with a quick kiss on the lips and pat on her behind. "You look freshly worked out with those flushed cheeks of yours," commented X. *If he only knew*, she thought. ○ was surprised at her own behavior and at how utterly normal she was acting in light of the fact that *she* was having an affair, while in full knowledge of the affair X had had with her best friend. What did she make of that? Was she psychotic? It was perplexing but too complex to rationalize at the moment.

The two of them shared pizza while reclining side-by-side on the sofa, an evening not unlike others they'd spent regularly over their seven-year marriage before there were secrets of infidelity to protect. But this time there was tension in the air. ○ was guarded and unable to relax.

X's movie choice generally won out over ○'s chick-flick favorites. Normally she gave in willingly because their time together cozying up on the couch was the highlight. Tonight, however, she wasn't as willing to give in, and so they compromised on a film that appealed to them both: *L.A. Confidential*. These were the happiest shared moments. Perhaps that was the best thing, if not the only thing, they did well together. Somehow it had seemed like enough, for a while ... until it wasn't.

The evening progressed like a treacherous mountain road in the night—filled with trepidation of what lie ahead at any given turn. At one point X gazed intensely over at O. He took her face in his hands and planted a long wet kiss directly on her mouth. O held her breath for fear that this would be the moment of truth, which would surely be followed by her own confession. But it wasn't. Throughout the film O kept wondering if X was suddenly going to come clean about his affair with B, and with every passing moment she questioned her own ability to stay true to herself.

In the end, O made no confessions about who she was really with that night at dinner, nor, needless to say, did she reveal her knowledge of X's affair with B. For once, she didn't betray herself. But her guilt sought attention, further stirring her angst. They were both protecting their secrets built around that night.

Would the truth ever come to light? O's constitution usually led her to confess. For her, keeping quiet was torturous. Sadly, keeping quiet came at a pricey bargain ... suffering inevitably ensued.

O 11

Two weeks had passed since O had last seen Mr. W. The email she'd sent him the afternoon after their talk expressing her continued devotion to his companionship and guidance, in spite of his shortcomings, had gone unanswered.

She was pensive as she walked down the hallways of the oncology wing, not knowing in what condition she'd find him and unsure of what to say. The smell of alcohol and disinfectant permeated the air, a scent O found comforting. Hospitals had their own unique presence, like something sacred.

O arrived on the sixth floor and promptly located Mr. W's room. "Knock, knock; may I enter?" she asked softly as she peered around the corner of the doorway. A weak voice sounded in response.

"Yes, yes, please do come in." Mr. W was sitting up in bed taking small bites of his evening meal.

"Hello, my dear, O. What a lovely surprise. Forgive me for not being appropriately dressed for your visit," he joked. At least he still had his sense of humor. He was thin and pale, and his once thick white mane of hair was gone. It was clear he was losing his battle with the cancer.

"Mr. W, it's good to see you sitting up and getting some nourishment in your system. I'm sorry it's taken me so long to visit," she apologized.

"No need to apologize. I'm still alive and kicking," Mr. W responded and then abruptly broke out in a coughing fit.

"How are you feeling, Mr. W?" The answer to that was obvious, but finding the right words with pending death staring you back in the face left one at a loss. His confession seemed almost trivial now. She'd always cared deeply for him, and her feelings were no different now.

"Well, I'm afraid I don't have much good news to report in that department. I'll be glad when it's all over. I'm so very tired," his voice trailing off.

Just then a fleet of doctors and nurses in white coats glided into the room. O moved out of the way, in awe of the powerful energy that filled the air. The head surgeon, his assistant, and seven doctors and nurses making their rounds surrounded Mr. W's bed as the assistant doctor gave a comprehensive report on Mr. W's condition. O stood silently in the background, observing. After several minutes they were gone again.

"O, my dear," W began with a tone of sincerity, "What you've just witnessed is God and his angels at work. They are everywhere roaming the hallways. You feel their presence when you enter the premises. *They* are the unsung heroes of the world. I should only be grateful to have the chance to witness such divinity on earth."

O was moved by Mr. W's words. He had changed during these last several weeks, not just because his physical body was dying, but also because the wisdom of his spiritual being was shining through.

"O, I've had a lot of time to think over the last several weeks," he said, taking her hand in his frail hands. "First, I thank you for the kind words you sent me. Over the years I've come to love you like my own daughter. Our talks were always a highlight of my day." Mr. W softly smiled as he took a thoughtful pause, reflecting on those many moments they shared together over tea or coffee in his office.

"What I want to say to you, O, is that the state of our world is dire. Every system on earth—environmental, social, cultural, political, and economical—is in the process of breaking down. The ways of man are no longer sustainable. The changes to come, and they

70

must come, will be global. Humanity is being given a major wake-up call. A global shift, if you will, is taking place that will lead either to self-destruction or to a new consciousness, a new way of life. If humanity doesn't change the way they relate to each other and the planet, I'm afraid it will be too late for our species. This may all sound quite dramatic, but it is a fact. We need a revolution, ○. A revolution to change everything we think we know about who we are and why we're here if we're to survive. Believe these words from a dying man." Mr. W closed his eyes and sighed deeply. Talking required too much energy.

"Mr. W, I understand your words. It is a frightening time to be alive."

"On the contrary, ○. It's a very exciting time to be alive. The future of the planet lies in the hands of every living being. This is indeed a historical event that is taking place right now."

○ let his words seep in. Mr. W had always been in touch with the big picture. Inherently, he was a futurist. It was exactly that talent which had led Blush & Company to success over the many years of his tenure.

"Mr. W, you need your rest. I should go now. Thank you for sharing your words of wisdom. I will take them with me and heed your warning."

"One last thing, ○," he whispered with the last bit of energy he could muster. "Follow your own path. Whatever happens, know that you are the master of your own universe. When faced with opposition, keep your faith alive. Know you will be fine. After all, Earth is the playground of our souls. Have fun and follow your deepest desires, no matter what. That is what really counts."

○ wasn't fully aware of the warning behind his words, or the importance of them to her future, but that too would soon be revealed.

The time had come for ○ to bid Mr. W goodbye.

That night Mr. W took his last breath.

O 12

It had been several weeks since O had spoken to B, though there were moments she wasn't sure she ever wanted to talk to her again. O grabbed the morning paper from the mailbox, put it under her arm and made her way to work in the morning traffic. O was sitting at her desk sipping her morning cup of coffee when her cell phone rang. It was X calling.

"Good morning, love," she answered.

"O, have you seen the paper today?" X asked impatiently.

"No, not yet—why?"

"Take a look at the front page headlines."

O unfolded the newspaper and read:

Medy Fined Millions for Fraud

"Holy shit! Have you spoken to B?" asked O.

"Yeah, just a few minutes ago. She's not in the office. I think you need to give her a call. It's serious."

"What about you? What's going on with you?" she asked apprehensively.

"I can't say right now. I'll let you know as soon as I know more. I've got to run. I'll see you at home tonight."

O hung up the phone and read through the rest of the article. DW was mentioned in connection to the case, but there was no direct mention of B, thank goodness. O had mixed feelings about calling B. She didn't know what to feel. Confusion was about all she could come up with. A strong cup of coffee and a few deep breaths should help bring clarity.

O paced anxiously back and forth in her office. Perhaps an S fix would give her more conviction. She wrote:

Dear S, hope you're having a good morning. Care for a quickie? ... No, no, scratch that. *Care to ... meet for lunch today at noon? Kisses, O.*

Oh, God, I shouldn't have done that, she immediately regretted. Courage mustered, she was now ready to make the call to B.

A faint voice answered the phone, "Hel ... lo?"

"Hi, B, it's me. I just saw the paper. How are you holding up?" O tried not to sound alarmed.

"Hi, O, love. I know it wasn't easy for you to call. I really appreciate it."

"So, what's the status with you and this whole mess?" asked O.

Trying to hold her tears at bay, B paused and took in a long breath before responding. It was clear she'd been crying and was on the verge of a nervous breakdown.

"Well, since I last saw you there was a hearing on the case. DW was there. The authorities have all our written documents from research, as well as secret documents between DW and myself. The truth is out. They know everything. The company will be fined millions for this, and we're being held accountable for the entire cover-up." B began to cry hysterically, no longer able to hold herself together.

"Oh dear; listen, B, why don't I come over? It'll be easier to talk in person." Before B could reply O was out the door.

O climbed in the car and had just stuck the key in the ignition when her phone rang. It was S.

"Hi, S, I see you got my message. Sorry for the short notice."

"I like spontaneity in a woman," he teased. "Lunch would be great. Why don't we do something simple at my place? That all right with you?"

O knew what that meant. "Precisely what I had in mind," said O, trying to hide her enthusiasm. "See you then."

With one eye made up, B answered the door in bright pink pajamas and matching furry thong slippers, her hair freshly crumpled by a hard sleepless night. She appeared confused, as though she didn't know whether to blow her nose or brush her teeth. O had reason to worry about her.

"Come in. Sorry, I don't look too good right now. It's the best I could do," B mumbled in a frail voice. Do you want something to drink?"

"No, no, thank you. Now, come over here, sit down, and tell me what's happened," O put her arm around B and led her over to the red loveseat in the living room.

"Well, like I said," she began slowly, "the authorities discovered the Phase III test results on our KiL drug that clearly indicated the deadly consequences if used under certain circumstances. DW knew this, but based on what he revealed to me, I didn't think this drug was high risk at all!" You know, O, there are a lot of drugs on the market that are dangerous, but people just don't know it. They get FDA approval for reasons that are sometimes unethical." B broke out again in a wail of tears. Gathering her composure, she continued.

"As I told you once before, our researchers discovered the drug was also effective against migraines. This was an exciting finding, but to get additional approval for this could likely take several more years. DW convinced me that we could get our sales team in on the good news and have them offer this to doctors as an additional benefit of the drug. With support from our corporate gift program for those who prescribed the drug, we had a sure winner. This resulted in millions of dollars in profit for us and made us all look like heroes."

"Wait a second," interrupted O. "What exactly is the corporate gift program?"

"That's our way of thanking our customers. They get such gifts as golf clubs, memberships, luxury holidays, cruises, etcetera. It's common practice in our industry," explained B, sounding a bit defensive.

"Okay, go on. Wait … X was part of your scheme then, wasn't he?"

"Yes." B fell silent for a moment. "He accepted the corporate gifts, but he was not totally gung ho in the beginning about using the drug for an unapproved purpose. He didn't know about the risks of the drug, of course, but I managed to convince him that it was well on its way to FDA approval for migraines. He eventually bought into the idea, thinking it would be a welcomed treatment for his patients. He had all good intentions, O. I'm to blame, not him."

"So, what happens to you, B?"

B began crying hysterically. "I … I've lost my job. I will never work in the pharma industry again. My record is tarnished for life. I'm doomed, O. I'm doomed. What do I do now?" B was crying so hard she was making herself sick.

O made her some herbal tea and put her to bed. "What will happen to DW?" asked O, wanting to know if the devil got his due, especially considering the fact that he had dragged B into this mess.

"He's been taken into custody."

"Ah, the price of greed," mumbled O.

Greed, ego—the downfalls of mortal man. Until they change, nothing will.

O made it back to the office in time to finish up her eyebrow presentation before lunch. It was nearly impossible to concentrate after her visit with B, and now she wished she hadn't made lunch plans so impulsively with S. In spite of everything, O still cared very much about B. They'd been long-time friends, which O didn't take lightly.

O13

O's pace quickened as she crossed the street to S's apartment. It was shortly before noon. The anticipation of her rendezvous with him was debilitating. Hunger was calling, but not for lunch.

S answered the door, twinkling as ever. What made him twinkle like that, O wondered, jealous of his energy. He looked positively irresistible in his black turtleneck and dress slacks.

"Come in, come in. I'm in the middle of sautéing," he said, rushing back to the kitchen. O followed behind, enjoying the rear view.

"Smells yummy. What's on the menu?" asked O, recognizing another one of S's talents.

"You are!" He spun O around toward him and planted a wet smooch on her mouth. His body was clearly ready for action. It burned for O in complement to her own. S slid his hands beneath her skirt, cupping her derriere in his palms and pressing her tightly against him.

"Wow, you don't waste any time," said O, somewhat surprised at his frontal attack.

"Yeah? Well, I've been waiting for this moment since I last saw you," S responded playfully. Then, in one quick, unpredictable move, he yanked down her pantyhose and spun her around to enter her from behind—no questions asked.

The shock of the maneuver caught O off guard, took her breath away. The sensation was life-saving, like medicine for the soul. Complete and utter satisfaction spilled its venom into her veins like a sweet, sweet poison, blurring her mind and sense of reality. It was literally a spiritual experience. Nothing could have been more delicious in that moment than receiving the pervasive scratch for the elusive itch she so desperately craved.

Just then, S's cell phone, which was sitting on the kitchen counter, began to ring. He let it … again and again. A palpable tension filled the air. Their excitement mounted … thrust, ring, thrust, ring, thrust, ring. With each ring S thrusted harder, until, unable to hold himself back any longer, he let out a loud moan of pleasure as his body released an explosion of energy and shuddered. He lingered in position a moment before slowly pulling himself out. Frozen in place while catching their breaths, they both took in the intensity of the moment, which left them tingling from head to toe.

"Now let's eat," pronounced S.

They sat down at the kitchen table, ready to enjoy the mixed green salad with sautéed mushrooms and homemade dressing. A silence fell between them. A strange feeling began to emerge within O. Something was missing in this encounter. Strange. What had just happened? O sat there, puzzled in reflection. Why did she suddenly feel like a whore? Their quickie, the very thing O had desired more than anything, was lacking something … emotional substance perhaps? But was that coming from him alone? What was she expecting anyway, a caring, loving relationship with meaning? Clarity eluded her. In an unconscious effort to overcome the growing feeling of meaningless sex, O attempted to establish some semblance of an emotional and intellectual bond with S beyond their sexual escapades.

"So, S, what's the status of things in your world? I mean, with the financial crisis and all. What's your take on things?"

"It's screwed, basically; what can I say? We've been earning damn good money. It was a real lucrative market for us bankers for a long time. We had control, and that my dear, is power!" he said, leaning in. "Those bonuses just rolled in every year like the lottery. What a shame; now the regulators want to put a stop to the bonus system that's been working so well for us for so long. That's really unbelievable. They even want to regulate our salaries! I tell you, this is getting out of hand. I want things back the way they were."

"But, S, things weren't working the way they were. That's why this crisis happened in the first place," argued O, stunned by his attitude.

"You're not in the banking business, my dear, so I don't think you fully understand the intricacies at work here. You're right to some extent that the system wasn't foolproof, but I believe we can regain control, with perhaps a few minor changes, without the interference of the regulators. Anyway, let's not spoil the incredibly sexy moment we just shared with talks of finance, shall we?" suggested S, nuzzling his nose up to hers. "I'd like to have you one more time for dessert," he whispered, grinning, with lust in his eyes.

O was taken aback by S's arrogance and belittlement of her intellect. That was enough to kill her libido. She thought back to the first time she had met him here in his apartment. There was something oddly empty about him. She was beginning to catch a glimpse of what that was. He was out of touch, emotionally deficient. Sex was for him, well … sex, a purely physical act. Apparently, he regarded his world of finance in the same emotionally detached way no matter who suffered in the end—get what you can for the glory of the money, feed the ego. But what did that mean to O in the end? Was the sex not stellar? Did it not quench the flame of desire, relieve her desperation, and scratch that itch? Has this confrontation put that now in jeopardy?

As the saying goes, be careful what you ask for—you just might get it … for better or for worse.

O¹⁴

X was on the phone when O walked through the door. She put her purse down on the hall table, the same place she'd found B's apartment key weeks earlier. That thought ran through her mind, among many others, as she hung up her coat and walked back to the bedroom to change into something more comfortable. She thought back on lunch with S in his apartment. As his character slowly revealed itself she was getting a nasty taste in her mouth. The question was, was she ready to walk away? Sex was needed, and he could satisfy her like no one else. Besides, there were no other candidates. Or were there? Was X still in the running? Of that she wasn't sure.

Physically, she was becoming aware of the price of deceit—stomach pains, lack of sleep, inability to concentrate at work, etcetera. There was no fooling her body or unconscious mind. They ruled. The biggest question was her marriage. Divorce came more and more frequently to mind, but the idea was fleeting. The thoughts didn't seem all too serious. In her heart she still loved X, in spite of it all. But something had to change.

"O, are you there?" called X from the living room.

"Yes, I'm just changing. Be right there." X was nursing a whiskey when O joined him on the couch.

"Tired?" he asked.

"Yeah. It's been an emotional day. I saw B today. She's not doing well at all. I'm really worried about her mental state.

"Me too," said X in a dark tone. "I think we need to keep a close eye on her."

"I think we need to talk about a few things, hon." O shocked herself. What the hell was she about to do? As always, she just never knew what was going to come flying out of her mouth. Self-betrayal was looming near.

"Right. I need to fill you in on the Medy case." X picked up on O's hint but not on the topic that was to follow. He took another sip of his whiskey and proceeded to explain. "I've been charged with malpractice," he said unemotionally.

"Good Lord!" gasped O.

"Hold on, hold on, don't go getting all worked up." X perpetually squelched O's emotions, an unconscious bad habit that served to irritate O to no end.

"Fortunately, my lawyer had a good argument. I was clearly misled. There was no evidence indicating my knowledge of the dangers involved with the KiL drug. I was also led to believe that the FDA had recommended the drug for use against migraines, so I can't be held accountable for prescribing it, since it was under false pretenses. The authorities dropped the malpractice charge, but I still have to pay a fine of five hundred thousand dollars. This will go on my record, but I'm free to continue practicing medicine." X let out a deep sigh of relief. He was glad to have the investigation over and verdict known. Though his story didn't quite match B's, she accepted his explanation without further inquiry.

"Thank God! What a relief!" exclaimed O, giving X a peck on the cheek. "Honey, that's a hell of a fine to pay, but I hope you'll avoid such practices in the future," scolded O. Taking in a deep breath, O addressed the next subject at hand.

"Honey, we need counseling."

"Counseling? What kind of counseling?"

"Marriage … sex counseling," answered O with great difficulty. Because she and X never discussed sex openly, it was a difficult subject to broach. The word *marriage* was a cover for what she really meant to say and finally managed to spit out. O naively believed if their sex problem were solved, their marriage would be back on track.

"I disagree. We're just having a dry spell. I've had a lot of stress at work with long hours. I just need a vacation." X's excuses were weak.

"Honey, it's nothing to be ashamed of. A lot of couples need a neutral sounding board to get over the dry period, as you call it. We haven't had a healthy sex life in years! This goes far beyond your excuses. Now, I'm happy to find someone who can help us, if you'll agree to go."

"Forget it! We can sort this out ourselves. We don't need help. In fact, we can start right now!" X pulled O down on the couch beneath him. He began to kiss her neck and fondle her breasts.

"Stop!" O struggled to free herself. He began tickling her, to the point that she could hardly breathe. "Stop!" she cried again through fits of laughter. "Let me go, I can't breathe!" she screamed, gasping for air.

X, fully amused and laughing with her, finally let her up off the couch. O readjusted her pants and sweatshirt as X grinned up at her. What a master he was at changing her mood. It was clear this discussion was over. What a waste of time.

The thought of having sex with X just hours after sex with S was completely unpalatable. She had wiggled out of it this time, but O knew she couldn't have it both ways. Was it worth letting go of S in order to patch up her marriage or was he still a possible future in spite of his emotional deficits? O had some serious decisions to make.

The twitch was back.

O15

The marketing department was gathered in the conference room for O's new product presentation. Her hair stood on end in anticipation of igniting their enthusiasm. It was her big day to shine. This was it; show-and-tell time. O was poised and ready to go.

"What makes this eyebrow enhancer so unique is the colored wax. It not only applies color evenly to each individual brow hair, but also adds beautiful definition and overall shape to the brows. And it lasts all day until you take it off. Application is equally as unique. This specially designed applicator allows for quick and even distribution of color. Unlike brow pencils, which require a careful hand to avoid uneven hard lines, this applicator gives a natural appearance. Additionally, to fulfill our new environmental standards I've just set forth for all new products, the packaging is made from bamboo."

"What's the price point for this product, O?" asked P, one of the members of the marketing team.

"Same as a good-quality mascara. I want it to be affordable to everyone, not positioned as an exclusive high-end product with a limited clientele," O responded emphatically.

There was a buzz of excitement among the team over O's new brow enhancer, with talk of it becoming one of Blush's best-selling products. After years of research and planning, O finally had this milestone on the marketing table. It was her baby, and she couldn't be more proud. This moment also served as a milestone in O's career and would hopefully make her a shoe-in for partner. The only sad note to this story was Mr. W. How she wished he could have witnessed its debut. He had been instrumental in placing her project as a priority in the research department.

O left the meeting with a feeling of elation, a welcomed contrast to the anxiety plaguing her psyche. Perhaps a few days off to clear her head and celebrate were in order. B suddenly came to mind. O hadn't heard from her in several days.

"Come on, B, pick up, pick up!" O was in the car on her way home as she attempted to reach B.

Where could she be? She always had her cell phone close at hand. That was how she managed to maintain her Love Goddess reputation. Last-minute requests were always in order. B was ready to respond at any given moment to help pacify the sexual desires of the next man in need. Suddenly a familiar male voice answered B's phone.

"Hello?"

"X? ... Is that you?" O was perplexed.

"O? Yes, it's me. I got an urgent call from B an hour ago and got to her place as fast as I could. She's taken an overdose of sleeping medication. I have to rush her to Emergency. Meet us there if you can."

O drove like a maniac to the hospital. What was this sinking feeling she had in the pit of her stomach? Why had B called X first and not her? Aside from the obvious medical support X offered, O was feeling overlooked. *I'm her best friend! Why didn't she call me first? I've always been there for her.* O was beginning to feel like a fool for having believed B when she'd said that their affair was over. Had wishful thinking deceived her again? What was the truth? Would she ever know?

Okay, O, get a grip! Such thoughts are only causing more undue stress, so knock it off! She yelled to herself over the blaring radio.

O arrived at the hospital the same time X did. B was unconscious as X rushed her into an examination room with O in close pursuit.

"B, B, can you hear me?" called X. He lifted her eyelids for any sign of consciousness and checked her vitals.

"We're going to have to pump her stomach," X said firmly to the two attending doctors. "O, I'm sorry, but you'll need to wait outside. I'll let you know her status as soon as I know more."

O reluctantly took her place in the waiting room, trying desperately not to feel shut out.

It seemed like hours before X emerged from the examination room. O jumped up from her seat to meet him halfway down the corridor.

"What's her status? Is she going to be okay?"

"Physically, she's going to be fine. Mentally is another story. It was attempted suicide, which she could try again," X explained with a heavy voice.

"Oh, dear God. Poor B. What can I do? What's the next step? Will she be able to go home?"

"She'll have to stay several days under observation in the psychiatric ward. Until then, I can't say much more. O, try not to get yourself too worked up over this, all right? She's out of danger for the time being and is in good hands. I'll let you know which room she'll be admitted to and when she'll be receiving visitors."

X was stoic in his response, as a good doctor often was, but in this case it was unnerving. O wasn't *just* another visitor. She wanted to matter. Feeling shut out was not an emotion she swallowed easily, but she had no choice in the matter.

The house was still … deafeningly quiet. Evening had fallen. O changed from her work clothes into her sweats and poured herself a glass of white wine. She sat motionless in the dark living room, listening to her eyes blink. Who even knew an audible sound could be heard from a blink, but there it was. O's thoughts and emotions were a mass of confusion, bouncing back and forth between the various relationships in her life. What was the root of their worth? She searched for deeper meaning beyond the suffering. O reflected on her life and the significance of recent events in the silence of the darkness.

The passing of Mr. W had left O feeling vulnerable at work without the support she'd become accustomed to over the years. Admittedly, his support served as a crutch of sorts. It was probably not good in the end, but Mr. W had helped her establish a reputation as a powerhouse of original ideas. It earned her respect … at least she thought so.

Then there was S. He scratched that perpetual itch. He made her feel alive, sexy and … and … empty. Yes, perhaps that was the reality she'd been avoiding. Empty, just like the feeling S radiated from the depths, or shallows of his being, as the case may be. Indeed, that itch got scratched, and boy, how fun that was in the making. But the affair, when she really thought about it, created an invisible stress all its own, which had gradually crept beneath her skin like a parasite. The question was which was worse, the itch or the parasite?

O slid off the arm of the sofa and walked over to the large picture windows. Parting the sheers, she peered out onto the dark street at the shadows the streetlights cast on the ground. A man stood at his open bedroom window smoking a cigarette—*another unconscious act of self-destruction*, O thought as she stared, lost in thought.

What about her husband? Was there a future in their marriage? Was she really happy? She loved X, but the question blazing through her mind was—is love enough? Is love enough? On closer examination of her feelings, O felt lonely, and if she was really being honest with herself, neglected—a word she'd grown to disdain. There was that same old theme all over again. Where was the exit to getting off this merry-go-round, she wondered.

O went to the kitchen to refill her wine glass as her thoughts switched to B, her best friend—or perhaps that was also a lie. She wasn't sure anymore. What was B's future, their future? The truth about her relationship with X may forever remain a mystery.

In an effort to break the silence and still her mind, O put on her favorite CD by The

Cars. She turned up the volume as the haunting lyrics to "Drive" spilled out into the dark room—lyrics that seemed to be telling ○ the truth about her own life at that very moment in time.

Emotionally drained, ○ lay down on the couch and covered her legs with the cotton throw that was draped over the back. Her eyes welled with tears. She was overwhelmed by anxiety and fear of the unknown.

The direction of ○'s life was uncertain, but one thing was for sure—change was in the wind.

With change must come acceptance … unless of course one prefers suffering.

Two days had passed since B's overdose when O finally received the okay for a short visit. X was already at work in the ward and was waiting for O outside B's hospital room to give her an update on her condition.

"B is awake. She's been diagnosed as clinically depressed. Please try and keep your visit brief, O. She's got therapy scheduled and shouldn't get too overwhelmed."

"I will," she promised. She quietly pushed open the door to B's room and went in.

"B … hi, how are you doing? Are you up for a visit?" asked O tenderly.

"Hi, O." B's voice was weak. "Yeah, sure, come in." She looked extremely pale and gaunt. For such a voluptuous woman full of energy, it was a disheartening appearance.

"How're you feeling, B?"

"Uh … I don't know. A bit stupid, I suppose," she admitted with sluggish speech and watery eyes. O sat down next to her on the bed and took her hands in her own.

"It's going to be fine, B. After a few days here you'll be feeling much better, and I'm sure you'll be able to go home. I'll be there to help you any way I can. I've got some time off," explained O, trying to comfort B as much as possible. B squeezed O's hand while reaching for a Kleenex to wipe her nose.

"I hope you're right, O. I—I just feel so lost. I can't help thinking about how I've hurt you." B relaxed back onto the pillow, her eyes groggy and unfocused. "X said he'd come stay with me when I got home," she mumbled as she drifted off into a light sleep.

O couldn't believe what she'd just heard come out of B's mouth. *X said what?!* O was stunned. Perhaps B didn't know what she was saying. Maybe she was too drugged to realize it. O rubbed her eye as the twitch began to resurface. Perhaps now was a good time to make her exit.

X was no longer on the floor and had gone back to whatever it was he needed to do.

O was dumbfounded, not knowing whether B was hallucinating or telling the truth. Would X have promised such a thing without saying a word to her about it? Could it have been something he said simply to calm her down?

O stumbled down the corridor, trying to make sense of things. After finding her car and climbing in, she could do nothing more than sit behind the steering wheel in a blank stare. She felt a thick veil shielding the truth about B and X. An urge for revenge began to grow. O was in need of a distraction. She pulled out her cell phone and messaged S in hopes of some reprieve:

"Care for a quick ... coffee?" The moment she hit send, remorse began to surface.

"Why on earth can't I just let this go? Am I so stupid, so weak that I have to go running to my lover for comfort?" Somehow S and the word *comfort* didn't belong in the same sentence, however. So what was it that S really gave her? O searched for an answer out of desperation to understand herself. After moments of reflection it suddenly seemed so clear. Indeed, it was the energy of feeling fully alive.

"Yes, that's it! Don't we all walk around half-asleep most of the time, numbed by life's routine? It takes something new, something even sinister to knock us over the head. Well, S really gave me a wake-up call. Perhaps that's what I ultimately craved. The exhilarating feeling of being truly *alive!*"

While waiting for S's reply, O decided to pass the time in town shopping—the proverbial cure for all that ails a woman's soul. Besides, she'd be in the vicinity of S's apartment, conveniently allowing for immediate gratification.

Three hours had passed, but the anticipated reply from S never came. O was beside herself. She went home, poured herself a glass of wine and sat in the darkness of the living room listening to her eyes blink—a routine that would never repeat itself ever again.

O 16

Over the next two weeks it became clear that B would not be leaving the psychiatric ward anytime soon. She was too unstable and still in danger of another suicide attempt. The conversation O had planned to have with X about his proposal to B was a moot point. B was as good as gone from both their lives, at least for now.

O was at the grocery store shopping for breakfast when her phone rang.

"Hello?"

"Hi, O, it's S. How are you?"

"Good, good," replied O, trying to sound cavalier, as though she wasn't still angry about being ignored over the last two weeks.

"Look, I'm sorry I never got back to you. Things are very tense here at the bank, and I've just got no time right now. I'm going to have to excuse myself for a while. Hope you understand."

"Of course, of course. No problem. I completely understand. Take care then."

"Yeah, you too, O."

So that was that—unceremoniously dismissed by Mr. S—short and sweet.

The painful withdrawal symptoms and depression ○ had anticipated upon the imminent end of her affair with S never actually surfaced. Indeed, and much to her surprise, ○ felt relief and a sense of freedom. Only then did she realize the full extent the stress of the relationship had had on her. All in all, ○ felt this to be a positive development in the scheme of things, provided she could keep the itch under control.

Over the coming months, as X and ○ made efforts to rekindle their passions, it became clear to ○ that their sexual relationship would never evolve from its current status. ○ continued in vain, however, to hope for a happy end and settled for the things that they'd always done well together—cuddling on the couch in front of the television or buying things that made them both feel like prosperous members of society. These activities may have actually kept the marriage functioning for a short while, but it was the never-ending nights out on the town that kept X out of their bed and left ○ feeling alone and neglected.

Oh yes, X loved ○ and ○ loved X, but that darned twitch just wouldn't go away. Until …

O17

It was 1:30 am when O woke the first time; X's place next to her in bed was cold and empty. She did her best not to run through the same old suspicions and worries that plagued her whenever he stayed out late. She did her best to go back to sleep. Finally, sleep came, but only for a short visit. She stirred again at 3:00. Still no sign of X. She did her best to hold the tears at bay, to avoid the upset, the hurt, the sadness rising inside her. She did her best not to lock him out.

At 5:00 he was still not home. O rose and paced the floor, trying to calm herself with reassuring words that never really did much good: "What's one more hour? What difference does it make if it's three o'clock or five o'clock when he gets home? Don't be so fixated on time," she scolded herself. But all her convincing was not able to extinguish the pain and frustration she suffered. O got back under the covers and prayed for sleep to show her mercy.

When O rolled over and glanced at the clock again it was 7:00 am. X was still not home. O was beginning to wonder if he'd show up at all, remembering the last time he blamed it on a card game and too much whiskey. Fueled by a feeling of complete helplessness, O threw back the bedcovers and jumped into her workout clothes. Opera was the only music powerful enough to compete with the fury of emotions pouring out of her as she ran in the cool morning air along the Mony River. ○ had reached this point on various occasions over the years, but this time something was different. There was a sense of finality to the decision that weighed on her mind and resonated in her soul. It was on this morning that ○ knew what she had to do with a sense of clarity that had eluded her throughout this long, painful journey toward the truth. Upon this very moment of realization, that darned annoying twitch, which seemed to have no rhyme or reason, disappeared … never to return again.

When ○ returned home X was passed out in bed. She jumped in the shower and got dressed. X slept. Filled with despair, ○ escaped in the car, driving to nowhere in particular. About half an hour away she stopped in Fai, a small suburb bordering the town of Home. She'd heard of its charm from friends but had never been there before.

Lost and not knowing in which direction to head, ○ began to wander down the main street of the small village, trying to repress the impatient tears forcing their way to the surface. A patch of dark clouds hung like a toupee in the sky over the town's center as a light rain began to fall.

○ turned down a narrow walkway to the left of the main street, where she came upon a sign at the edge of a dirt path that read *The Path of Hope*. Well, either the universe had a great sense of humor, or there really was such a thing as fate. A tear escaped its hold as she blinked up at the sign in disbelief. She followed the path up a steep hill and stopped in a clearing surrounded by tall pine trees. A wooden bench stood beneath their outstretched limbs, inviting her to sit. ○ obliged. She sat and felt the stillness of her being. Then, from the depths of her soul, the bottled-up emotions, accumulated over years of denial and unfulfilled yearnings, released themselves until there were no more.

Drained and exhausted, ○ dried her eyes and made her way back down the hill. There was a For Sale sign in the yard of a small cottage-style house off to the right of the path. They were having an open house. She decided to explore.

The house had been built in the early fifties and was extremely well kept, with a small garden in the back, hardwood floors, and two bedrooms off the living room and dining room. The kitchen was large with a breakfast nook in the corner. ○ had a funny feeling about it. It seemed almost familiar in some odd way. She left with the realtor's information in hand.

The synchronicity of life has a language all its own.

O18

How do you leave someone you love? A wrenching dichotomy of emotion tore at her heartstrings as she placed the freshly written note on X's pillow and left their house for the last time. The keys to her new home were clenched in the palm of her hand. *How ironic,* she thought as S suddenly crossed her mind … to leave the one you love and need the one you don't.

That night as O lay sleeping, an insight, a sense of knowing, came to her. It seemed to come forth from a source outside herself:

Sex is the symbolic expression of both the physical and spiritual bodies. It is the gateway to nirvana, next to godliness, and is the highest expression of joy one soul can share with another. It is the bridge to a higher state of consciousness and the physical experience of the universal truth— we are all one. It is to be celebrated, not denied. It's as natural as the comings and goings of the ocean's tides. It is energy in need of expression, connecting the spiritual with the physical realms. To deny sex is to deny self-nourishment, which leads to a withered soul.

Like an epiphany, it grew slowly into a sense of absolute knowing and served to comfort the very thing O had struggled with throughout her marriage—the denial of her own sexual needs. In that knowing she recognized the gift and soul value of the affair with S.

Indeed, he was a gift she'd given to herself—one born out of need but created out of a deeper, unconscious knowing.

With this newfound understanding, ○ found forgiveness for herself.

O19

O's drive to work, though thirty minutes longer, was of little consequence. She was the proud owner of a new home, and life was taking a new direction. It reflected a style contrary to past choices and was indicative of her need for a renewed sense of self-expression. Being alone had its simple pleasures and allowed her time to experience, perhaps for the first time, a glimmer of belief in herself.

After arriving at the office and engaging in the morning paper, the phone rang. Mr. C was calling.

"Good morning, Mr. C. What can I do for you?"

"Good morning, O. Uh … there is a matter we need to discuss. Could you come to my office, please?"

"Yes, of course. I'll be right there." *Hmm*, she thought, tapping her fingers on the desk. O was certain she knew what the discussion would be about. The chairman was thrilled about the new eyebrow enhancer and wanted to offer his kudos, though it was difficult to picture him thrilled about anything but money. He didn't give praise easily, but when he really liked something, meaning when he could smell the profits, he could be quite gracious.

When ○ arrived at his office, one of the other board members, Mr. G, was already present.

"Thank you for coming, ○," said Mr. C, a big man in every sense of the word, as he motioned ○ over to the armchair in front of his desk. "I hope I haven't interrupted any important meetings you might have had arranged this morning?"

"No, not at all," ○ replied, sitting down in anticipation of the praise to follow.

"○, your new eyebrow enhancer is quite impressive. This could be very lucrative for us. There're just a few legal details about the formula and packaging that need to be worked out, but it's well on its way to market."

○ was pleased with herself. "Thank you, sir. I think this could become one of our best-selling products."

"Yes, indeed," he nodded. "There is, however, another reason for me asking you here today," Mr. C added, taking a thoughtful pause. He got up from his chair and sat on the corner of his desk before ○ as she listened intently. Thoughts of a promotion crossed her mind.

"○, we are going through a restructuring of the company. We must consider the current economic environment, you understand. This restructuring will cause a few positions to become redundant. I regret to say yours will be one of them."

○ blinked several times, unsure of whether she'd heard Mr. C correctly or not.

"Excuse me?" she said in a surprised voice. "Could you please repeat that, Mr. C?"

"I'm terribly sorry, ○. But we have no choice but to let you go."

"What? What! I don't think I understand! I've just created one of the most innovative products Blush & Company has seen in years, and you're laying me off? I really don't believe this. This can't be true!" ○ jumped up out of her chair and began to pace the room, her pulse racing. The words of Mr. W flashed through her mind. They had seemed to hint at some obscure change. But she had never taken them to mean this.

"Now, ○, take a deep breath and calm yourself. These things happen all the time, particularly in today's financial environment. It's happening everywhere to many other companies, not just ours. It cannot be avoided."

"With all due respect, Mr. C, I have dedicated myself to this job, offering my best ideas, and have given this company many successful products that are still performing well on the market. I've accumulated numerous hours of overtime for which I've not been compensated, but I have graciously offered them. I have been loyal and worked for the good of all in this company. How could you just let me go?"

"O, I'm very sorry. You will be given a fair severance package and a high recommendation from us. We thank you for your loyalty, but sometimes it just comes down to this." Mr. C's words were final. There was no amount of convincing or arguing that could change his decision.

O walked in a daze back to her office, numbed by the event. It was all so surreal. Mr. C's words still reverberated in her ears: "… will cause a few positions to become redundant."

This can't be … this can't be! What have I done to deserve this? Why is this happening to me? What is going on with my life? O reviewed the list of recent events: a new mortgage, a lost job, a lost husband, a lost best friend, and a lost lover. *And now … what do I do? Will I have to give up my new home? Will I end up on the streets?*

O was sinking into a deep, dark hole. Life had stripped her of everything she held dear, particularly her security. Her future now lay in her own two hands.

In pain and in loss the whole is greater than the sum of its parts.

◯20

Standing in the middle of her living room, fists tightly clenched, ◯ let out a loud, gut-wrenching primal yell from the depths of her soul.

"*Noooo!* I won't give in to this! I won't give in to *fear*. I refuse to let it make me small! I won't let it paralyze me. There must be a greater purpose in all this. There *must* be!"

Panting from the force of her will, sunlight streaming in through the windows across her face, a quiet calm took over her being. The air felt naked around her. She let out a long exaggerated breath as she felt herself letting go—letting go of everything she'd ever resisted and fought against—change, disappointments, denial, fear. She found herself aligning with an energy that began to flow into her consciousness. It grew slowly into a sense of purpose and possession over her life. Mr. W's words of inspiration echoed in her ears: "*Follow your own path. Whatever happens, know that you are the master of your universe.*"

Was she the owner of these thoughts that suddenly began to stream into her mind? *Life is of my own creation. Nothing is random. There is a purpose to all things. It's my perspective that's wrong. These events only appear to be setbacks. I'm not being led into doom, but rather toward that which I desire.*

"I *deserve* good things to come to me!" ◯ shouted as a new sense of self-worth, the very thing she'd struggled with throughout her life, began to evolve within her and strengthen with each affirmation. "I have to believe that. I do believe that. I have a greater purpose in my life that I've yet to discover. I will find it out, and I won't quit until I do."

That moment gave rise to an even greater insight, one she'd never considered before:

Hidden within every event, every experience of her life was a divine message. From the twitch to the itch, from the ring to the scratch, Life was speaking to ○ through her denials and her sufferings with these symbolic wisdoms.

○ became aware of the miracle at work: how each event in her life served as guidance, how each message was a learning waiting to be discovered. And she, like alchemists changing lead into gold, could change perceived disadvantages into advantages. ○ suddenly realized the irony that neglect—her nemesis—played in her life. It was that very thing that saved her in the end, for self-worth and neglect go hand in hand. Life had challenged ○ to discover her self-worth by giving her the opposite of that experience. Life was reflecting back to her that which she denied herself. It was neglect that finally broke her, that finally led her to make the agonizing decision to end her marriage. It was only out of complete desperation and suffering that ○ had been enabled to honor herself and her needs in the end. Sadly, such was the unconscious state of the human condition—learning through suffering.

X's real role in ○'s life suddenly began to emerge in her consciousness. In as much as he seemed not to give—he gave beyond boundaries. At a soul level, he was willing to give up his love for her for the evolution of her own soul. The opportunity to evolve was grace in disguise and his soul's gift to her future.

Life masterfully scripted every detail, like pieces to a puzzle, every piece fitting together in perfect harmony from which the stories of her life unfolded.

The duality of human existence—to play both the actor and the audience simultaneously—is the challenge that we as spiritual beings in a physical realm endeavor to experience. In other words, learning to step out of the story of our lives and see the miracle of life as it shows us who we really are through life itself. Such wisdom has the power to end suffering.

A sense of peace filled ○'s heart like a warm flame. From her deepest sense of knowing, ○ knew she would be all right. The proverbial dragon of fear had finally been slain. Though she wasn't sure of the source of this renewed sense of faith, desperation had forced her to rise to the occasion. It was showing ○ her true self and bringing forth a part of herself she'd never encountered before.

She felt oneness with the All, of this earth and beyond, in this dimension and in others. The feeling was a familiar one. It was the feeling of universal love. Her will gave rise to conviction.

"From this moment forward, fear no longer exists for me. There is no past. There is no future. There is only the powerful moment of *now*. This is where my life begins. This is how I shall move forward."

○ knew she would take up contact with B again at some point, but for now, B needed time to heal. As for X, he would continue to be a part of ○'s life but in a capacity of her choosing. Her love for him would never die.

○ was heading on a new life's journey, which would reveal its mysteries every step along the way. A new chapter was about to begin …

AFTERWORD

The story of ◯ and the theme of neglect serve as metaphors for the current state of the human condition. It is the neglect of our souls and our planet that's in need of attention. Change beckons. Living conscious lives is the cure to end all suffering.

O DEFINED

[O] Original origin; the source and the life of all things; the universe and all that is; the symbolic ring of union connecting all existence to the One; the beginning and the end of the never-ending cycle of life.